AFTERMATH

by

BARBARA M. HODGES

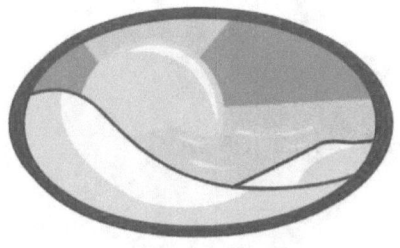

Coastal Dunes Publishing

187 Alyssum Circle
Nipomo, CA 93444
Coastaldunespublishing.com

Author's Note

This book is a work of fiction. Names and characters are used fictitiously, and any resemblance to actual persons is coincidental.

Acknowledgments

Authors sometimes feel we write alone. That is so un-true, so to my mom, Jean, my husband Jeff, the Santa Maria, California Word Wizards, and everyone else who has been a part of my writing journey, thank you, thank you, and thank you.

Barbara M. Hodges

Books
by
Barbara M. Hodges

ICE CO-WRITTTEN WITH RANDOLPH TOWER

ONE LAST SIN-CO-WRITTEN WITH RANDOLPH TOWER

A SPIRAL OF ECHOES-CO-WRITTEN WITH MAGGIE PUCILLO

SHADOW WORLDS-CO-WRITTEN WITH DARRELL BAIN

THE BLUE FLAME

THE EMERALD DAGGER

THE SILVER ANGEL

AFTERMATH

Table of Contents

Child of Prophecy......Page 6
Rainbow Raindrops...Page123
The Golden Avatar....Page 134

The Child of Prophecy

Prologue

Mirabella Passed Her hand over the wavering water in the shallow scrying bowl.

"*Aura...maren...serenus*, gentle breeze of the sea calm." The surface flattened and a shroud of fog formed and hovered above the water. "Doorway of mist part. Heed the call from the blood of the Ancient and show me who I seek." A wind flowed from the corners of the cottage, parted the white mist and she stared into a kitchen.

Rays of sun streamed through pristine panes of glass and glistened off counters of white tile. Planter boxes outside the window burst with rosemary, thyme and basil.

A petite woman, her pale hair pulled back and secured at the nape of her neck with a tortoise-shell clip, sat at small table, her head bent over an open book. Suddenly she shivered looked upward and rubbed her bare arms.

Her brow wrinkled in puzzlement.

Mirabella nodded with a pleased smile of recognition. Eleanor. It has been a long time, and in this life you are a woman of mature years. Good, even untrained you feel me.

She waved her hand again across the water of the scrying bowl. "Now, show me the messenger."

She could see trees, a gray path. "Who...?"

The scene narrowed until but one running man filled the bowl. He slowed to a walk. The man was tall, with a shaggy mane of hair black as a

moonless night. He wore a sunshine-yellow, shapeless top and gray, baggy pants. His tanned skin glowed in the early morning light.

He stopped, turned his smoke-blue eyes upward and Mirabella smiled. "Ah, of course, Mason Warren. Now I understand. Open to me, Mason, and hear my words."

Chapter One

Brianna Sang Along with the oldies station as it played *Into The Mystic* by Van Morrison. As the song faded, she spooned another mound of fudge icing on top of the pan of brownies, smoothed it, and then created some delicate swirls. She stepped back with a satisfied smile. The icing was a good half-inch deep, just like she loved it. "You can never have enough chocolate."

Some oozed over the edge of the pan, and she wiped it free with her finger. She sampled the creamy icing with her tongue and sighed in pleasure.

The front door buzzer sounded and she glanced at the clock. 8:40, she didn't open for another 20 minutes. "Damn, can't anybody read?"

She wiped her hands on a towel, called. "I'll be right there. You're early."

Her gaze swept across the three frosted cakes that still waited to go into the display case. She picked up the Black Forest, adjusted a cherry, and went through the two white swinging doors and out into the front of the bakery.

Her early customer was a man. A jogger from the looks of his yellow tee shirt and gray sweat pants. His long, black ponytail surprised her. You didn't see that much around Santa Theresa, must be a tourist from Los Angeles.

She gave him her best customer-smile. "Good Morning. Beautiful day, isn't it?"

He said nothing for a moment, just stared at her with his smoke-blue eyes. His gaze made her

conscious of the damp strands of hair that clung to her forehead and her cheeks warmed. Well, if he wasn't twenty minutes early, I would've had time to comb my hair and put on some lip-gloss. She turned away from him and bent to place the cake into the case.

"The name hooked me, Java Jive's Bakery." His voice was dark, like his hair. "Am I too early? I saw the lights on."

She straightened and smiled again. "Catchy name, isn't it? The special today is a mocha latte and a blackberry scone. What can I get you?"

"Sounds great." He smiled, showing even, white teeth.

"For here or to go?"

"Here, please."

She waited for him to go to one of the tables, but instead he picked up one of her new business cards off the counter. "This is a nice place. It's very down-home. I like the red geraniums. They were my mom's favorite flower."

She bristled as she swept her gaze across the bakery. Down-home? She'd been hoping for Paris chic. The green, granite counter had been her biggest expense and the reason she'd had to opt for the geraniums in the terra cotta pots for each table.

"Really," she said with forced pleasantness. "How nice."

He pointed to the framed decorative tiles hanging upon the walls. "I have some like them in my pool house."

Yeah? Then why don't you go home and dunk your head in your fancy pool and forget to breathe. Her thoughts must have shown upon her face, because a slight frown wrinkled his sun-browned

forehead.

"Will there be anything else?" she said quickly.

"Another one of those blackberry scones to go."

"I'll be right out with it." She kept her smile plastered in place until he turned and walked to the nearest table and then released a deep breath. Upsetting your first customer. Not a good way to start your day, Brianna.

She put his mocha latte together and then placed one still warm scone on a pale-green china plate and the other in a white paper bag. Maybe that would smooth things.

He was still giving the bakery a good once over as she walked toward him, and she frowned. Was he shopping for a local business? Well, it wasn't going to be hers. She wouldn't be a millionaire anytime soon, but....

"You never get tired of that smell, do you?" he said.

The words threw her. "What?"

"Cinnamon and sugar, my grandma's kitchen always smelled like this." He pulled out a chair and sat down. "Do you bake gingerbread, too?"

"Only during the holidays." She placed the scones and coffee before him. "I've got some peanut butter cookies in the oven. I'll be in the back for the next few minutes." She turned away, but his next words stopped her.

"Are you the Brianna Cole listed here?" He held the card out toward her.

"That's me."

He nodded. "I'm Mason Warren. Could you sit down for a minute?" He indicated the chair across

from him.

She recognized his name, but from where?

Brianna waved a hand toward the back of the bakery. "I'm really very busy..."

"Take care of your cookies," he said and leaned back. "I'll wait."

"Mister Warren, if this is about Java Jive. It isn't for sale. Try Pismo Beach, the next town north of here."

"It's nothing like that. I'd like to hire you. I need a caterer. The card says you cater." He tapped the card on the table. "I was going to let my fingers do the walking, but...it must be magic, me coming in here."

She smiled at his choice of words. The buzzer on the oven sounded. "Give me a minute."

Her heart beat fast as she pulled the cookies from the oven. My first catering job. She set the cookies on the large table and went back to the front of the shop.

"What kind of party?" she said.

"Halloween."

Her stomach did a dive. "That's two days away."

"I know."

"Sorry," she said with a shake of her head.

"Wait, hear me out.

She pressed her lips together. She didn't want to hear him out. He'd dangled a nice carrot in front of her for a nanosecond and then jerked it back.

"Look." He handed her a sales invoice. "Read this."

It listed: 25 lbs. of cracked crab, 20 lbs. of shrimp, all the fixings for cocktail sauce, every kind of booze made, six kinds of beer, two cases of

assorted wines, and another three cases of champagne. Three smoked hams and two smoked turkeys. The list ended with ten or twelve different cheeses and every variety of crackers she'd ever heard of and a couple she hadn't.

"Are you feeding an army?" she said.

"Around 100 guests."

She still shook her head. "Super woman I'm not. I'd need a week to turn this list into food...."

"I have a staff...well, the other caterer's staff."

She had to ask. "Why don't you have the caterer?"

"He had a family emergency. His daughter was in a car accident."

"Oh, my God."

"She'll be okay, but he had to go to Boston. Now I have all the food ordered, the use of his staff, but I need someone to pull it all together."

Brianna frowned. "How many on his staff?"

"Ten. Three bartenders and seven others to help set up, prepare, and serve. All very experienced."

"In two days. I don't know." She tried to wrap her mind around the problem.

"I'll double what I was paying him, that's six thousand dollars."

She took a deep breath. She could buy the new Hobart mixer she'd had her eyes on and even take a weekend trip to San Francisco. She looked up and met his intent gaze. He wasn't stupid; he knew she was thinking it over.

He leaned toward her. "If it goes as well as I think it will, I'll even throw in a five hundred dollar bonus."

That's enough to replace the espresso

machine. It's too good. I can't turn it down. "Okay, I'll do it."

"Great." He picked up a napkin, wrote on it and handed it to her. "Directions to my house."

"River's Rush," she said. "Arthur Hanson's place. I'd heard there'd been a buyer."

"You know it." Not a question.

"I've never been up there, but yes, I know it." She looked harder at him. "So you're the mystery man."

He smiled. "You know of me?"

She shrugged. "People talk."

"What have you heard?"

"Odd-ball, recluse, a mafia hit-man on the lam, I've heard them all. Small towns, you know," she said with a shrug.

"I'm plain old Mason Warren," he said. "Looking for a little peace and quiet."

Then it came to her where'd she'd seen his name, but he didn't look much like the austere man in the photo plastered all over the front of yesterday's Santa Theresa Times. Self-made millionaire and single. They'd dubbed him the Wall Street Wizard; it seemed what he touched turned to gold. "I'll need two hours to set up."

"I'll expect you at seven o'clock and make sure the rest of your staff is notified also." He stood. "And, by the way Miss Cole, this is a costume party, Elizabethan era."

She grimaced. "I'll see what I can do."

"Then I'll say thank you and get out of here before you change your mind."

She watched until he walked out the door and then shook her head. What have I gotten myself into?

Chapter Two

Brianna Slowed And edged to the right of the narrow blacktop road. As she glanced down again at the directions, a horn blared behind her. "Okay. Sorry." She looked at the green illuminated numbers of the clock and frowned. Shit, I'm already late. The directions had seemed simple, but she'd lost twenty minutes when she'd taken the first turn, Mountain Crest Circle, instead of Mountain Crest Loop.

A little further down the road, she saw the street sign as she passed. "Damn."

It took her another mile before she found a place wide enough to whip a U-turn.

She took a deep breath and forced herself to loosen her death grip on the steering wheel. Hey, I'll get there when I get there.

She spied Mountain Crest Loop, made the turn and looked for the rusted wagon wheel mentioned in the directions. "There." She slowed. His directions said the driveway would be soon. Her headlights cut across a stone cairn with large, metal numbers. "Yes." She made a quick right turn.

The road twisted, climbed upward. Evergreens crowded close. A narrow, planked bridge crossed a wide chasm and even through the closed windows she heard the roar of rushing water. I wonder what this place looks like in the daylight? Must have quite a view. She rounded a curve and slowed. White moonlight flooded a wide expanse of

green grass. Topiaries in fanciful animal shapes surrounded the lawn; a rabbit tipping a hat, a rearing unicorn, and a dragon with wings wide for flight. In the wash of light, they seemed a moment away from breathing.

Brianna looked across a wide expanse of manicured lawn. Her eyes widened in astonishment. You couldn't call what she viewed a house, it didn't fit. It was huge, some dark color, and built on the form of a geodesic dome. The closest thing she could compare it to was a giant egg. A widow's walk circled its middle like a narrow belt. The gothic walkway looked out of place on the modern mound of architecture. Oval windows, like dark eyes, were spaced across its front.

With a deep sigh, she parked her aging Toyota next to a new red Mazda Miata. There were seven other cars there with the Miata. It was too early for the guests. They must belong to the rest of the caterer's staff.

She glanced at the house and saw a figure on the widow's walk. It moved into the moonlight. It was too far away for her to see who it was, but a certainty hit her. It's him, Mason. He loves the night, always has. The thought made her shiver. How can I know what Mason Warren likes? Before yesterday morning they'd never met.

He circled the dome, stopped above the front door and stared toward her.

He can't see me. It's impossible. But she felt her stomach tighten. Brianna climbed from behind the steering wheel. She closed and locked the car door. When she looked up again, he was gone.

Chiding herself for her over-active imagination, she hurried toward the front door.

Aftermath

White paper-bag luminaries lined the curving sidewalk and the wide flagstone entry-way. As she lifted her hand to push the bell, the door swung inward. The smell of burning candles and musky incense hit her nose.

Mason had chosen a monk's costume, all in black. A gold chain belt circled his waist. A smaller chain hung around his neck, and suspended from it was a ruby the size of a pigeon's egg.

Elizabethan? Well, she supposed a monk was a monk no matter what era. She grinned as she saw the white toes of a pair of running shoes peaking from beneath the robe's hem. She wore a pair of Nikes beneath her own get-up.

"Welcome to my home, Brianna."

"Thank you, Mr. Warren."

She watched his gaze take in her cream-colored peasant blouse and rust-red, floor-length, full skirt. "It's the best I could do at such short notice."

"It suits you, and please, make it Mason," he said. "I'm sorry you got lost."

A chill touched the back of her neck. "How did you know I'd gotten lost?"

His eyes narrowed for a moment before he smiled. "You are thirty minutes late. Very unlike you, I'm sure. What else could it have been?" He took her arm and drew her forward. "Come, I'll show you to the kitchen and introduce you to the rest of the catering staff."

The kitchen shone bright beneath overhead lights. Expectant faces turned toward her, then hands were outstretched and names given.

"How many guests," she asked Mason as he handed her a glass of iced tea.

"Herbal. Raspberry with two sugars, like you prefer it," he said.

Taking it from him, her eyes widened."Don't look so surprised. I always check out anyone I hire. The guest list is small," he went on. "Just over a hundred." He motioned to a man who stood in the shadows. "Chad, this is Miss Cole. She will be in charge of the food for this evening. Miss Cole, this is my chef."

A white-clad man with black creased skin like a raisin appraised her with chocolate-colored eyes. He nodded with a tight smile. Great. He's territorial. She held out her hand to him. "I'm glad you're here. It'll make it much easier to work with someone who knows the kitchen."

Chad's poker-stiff body relaxed a little at her words.

"I left some things in my car. If…."

Two young men jumped forward, their shoulders colliding. "We'll get them for you."

"Why, thank you." She dropped her keys into the nearest hand. "Now, if you will show me the refrigerator, Chad, we can get started.

*****

Brianna stood against the wall and looked around. A door had been opened between two rooms to make this one the size of a small amphitheatre. A ten-piece orchestra played at the far end. Her three tables and a fully stocked bar sat at the opposite end. In between the two, people milled, a few danced, but most chatted in small groups. She counted nine Henry VIIIs, seven Queen Elizabeths, eleven Robin Hoods, and twelve Maid Marions, scads of lords and ladies and hoards of bar maids, their peasant blouses sliding halfway off

17

their shoulders to bare lots of cleavage. She glanced down at her own top to make sure she wasn't guilty of the same.

The heady scents of exotic perfumes, spicy aftershaves, and candle wax hung heavy in the air. It was the incense of pleasure, and she inhaled it greedily.

Her gaze drifted around the room, grinning at the Transylvanian decor. Black tapers in gleaming silver candelabras circled the room. The guests' shadows danced along the walls as they moved in and out of the light. Their cavorting images reminded her of a live theatre presentation of Dante's Inferno.

Three adult-size skeletons with red carnations glued to where collars would lie open, and all wearing black top hats, hovered in dark corners. Cobwebs floated around recessed lights and a yellow orb of a harvest moon hung in its golden glory in the ceiling's center. In the middle of the moon, blood dripped from a huge bat's fangs.

It was cheesy, crass, and she loved it.

What kind of man is Mason Warren? The write-up in the paper said he'd moved from New York City, and that he'd made millions in the stock market. So why is he here in Santa Theresa?

"Everything is wonderful. How can I thank you, Brianna?"

She jumped and gasped at the words whispered so close to her ear. "I don't know if I did your décor justice," she said in a rush.

Mason grinned. "I know it's a little much, but I gave Roman free reign and this is what I got." He pointed to one of the Robin Hoods complete with longbow and quiver of arrows. "He's my assistant. I

would have gone with black-and-orange crepe paper, but he insisted gothic ala Dracula would be expected."

She looked again at his black robe and smiled. "Did he choose your costume, too?"

"Mine? No, it was my choice. Too much, do you think?"

Her face heated and she was glad to see one of the staff motion to her from a doorway. "Excuse me. Duty calls."

Mason stared as she moved away. *She doesn't remember me.*

He'd been surprised to see her when she came toward him from the back of the bakery. He'd known his forever love was in Santa Theresa; there could have been no other reason for the pull he'd felt toward the small town, but to find her this soon? *Thank you, Goddess.*

She hadn't changed much, his Eleanor, a little older in this lifetime and with darker hair. Had Mirabella known of their past when she'd chosen him to go to Brianna? Of course she had. She'd said Brianna was the one who'd make the difference in the light or the dark winning the war simmering in Alamonar, but she hadn't gone into why, saying only all would be explained when they were together.

Watching Brianna prepare for the evening had fascinated him. Like a cyclone of energy she whirled from one end of the room to the other, touched down, added something here, suggested less there, always with a calm voice and sweet smile of reason. Tables appeared, seemingly having jumped into position already spread with pristine white cloths. Silver bowls of punch, and others mounded with pink shrimp on mountains of ice were wheeled from

the kitchen.

She'd carried out a tray, almost as big as she was, that brimmed with delicate canapés. Small engraved goblets filled with crab cocktails filled one table.

Shrill laughter grated on his ears and he turned to survey his guests. He knew their names, business acquaintances, all of them, not one would he consider a friend. When had he last had a friend? Not in this lifetime, he was certain of that.

The area in front of the hosted bar was popular. Golden champagne bubbled down a tower of glasses. Every variety of alcohol flowed as well as bottles of water, soda and never-empty urns of coffee. He'd arranged for the local cabbies to start making their appearances at midnight. The staff had strict instructions to keep an eye out for those who'd overindulged and, if noted, car keys were to be taken, one way or another.

He heard the crash of breaking glass, followed by a strident laugh and watched Brianna rush by him. For a quick, unguarded moment, he saw her tense mouth and creased forehead before her smile jumped back in place.

He watched her sweep up the shattered glass, and then followed as she scurried toward the kitchen.

With a sigh, she rubbed at the back of her neck and then massaged her temples. She turned toward him, swayed, and reached out for a counter top.

"When did you eat last?" She looked blankly at him, and he swore beneath his breath. He guided her to a chair as a young woman came into thekitchen. "Bring me one of those crab cocktails,"

he ordered. "And a bottle of water." The girl hurried away and returned moments later. Mason pushed the water into Brianna's hands. "Drink."

"No. I'm fine. I have to..."

"Everyone can survive a few minutes without you. If I see you back out there before thirty minutes has passed I'll withdraw my offer of a bonus."

Brianna gave him a quick salute. "Yes, sir."

A young man came into the kitchen.

"You," Mason said. "What's your name?"

"Mike."

"Well, Mike, you're in charge of the catering for the next thirty minutes. Can you handle it?"

"Sure," Mike said. "There's nothing to do but fill bowls or plates."

With a long look at Brianna, Mason turned and walked out the kitchen door.

With a sigh she took another long drink of water. He was right she did need a break.

One of the catering staff came in. "We need more shrimp."

Brianna started to stand. "It's behind the..."

"I know where it is," Mike went over and opened the large refrigerator.

She cringed and came to her feet as she heard the ring of crystal bowls striking each other. She'd never last thirty minutes if she didn't get out of this kitchen.

She walked to the door and turned left, away from the sound of laughter and rising voices.

Brianna welcomed the quiet hallway she walked. A few steps ahead a slash of light leaked from beneath a closed door. Without hesitation she

moved toward it. Her hand grasped the doorknob and for a moment she wondered why she felt no guilt at her brazen action. With a shrug, she opened the door.

The room was a softly-lit art museum. Her feet sank into a deep, plush, red carpet as she entered. She walked toward a marble statue of an angel. Her fingers traced its cool ivory cheeks as she breathed a soft, "oh," of pleasure.

She wandered deeper into the room, past a suit of armor and then another marble statue. Her gaze swept across an oil painting and then jerked back. No, it couldn't be. It just looked the same. Her breath caught in her throat as she looked for and then found the tiny ground squirrel's head in the far left-hand corner of the landscape.

The scene was a forest glen. Tall trees ringed it and blue-and-yellow wildflowers dotted an open field. The foreground held a fallen log and a woman sat on it her back to the viewer. Her plaited, gold hair shimmered and she wore a simple dress of sky-blue with a white apron tied at her waist. Beside her on the log was a basket full of flowers. Her head was cocked as if she listened to, or for, something. And there was the curious little ground squirrel.

Brianna knew if the woman turned she would have blue eyes.

"Who are you?" she whispered. She looked for the signature of the artist and found none. Unwilling to move away, she lowered herself to the floor. Her gaze moved across its surface. Yes, even the brown and black knothole next to the woman's hip was the same. A sweet scent teased her nose and she yawned. I should get back to the kitchen. She leaned back against the wall and closed her eyes. A

minute more, then I'll go back.

*****

Mason stood on the widow's walk. On the horizon sheet lightening slashed across the black ink of night. "One...two...three..." He counted seven before the rumble of thunder sounded. As agreed, Mirabella had waited until the last of his guests crossed the bridge before she called down the storm. A blast of frigid wind molded his robe to him, and he felt the first drops of icy rain. He tilted his head back and opened his mouth. The rain tasted sweet on his tongue, ripe with magik.

Then the storm was upon him. Rain pelted his body. In one smooth movement he pulled the robe over his head and dropped it on the walk. Skyclad, he raised his arms toward the boiling clouds and chanted into the wind. Three times he walked a small circle, the volume of his words rising with each step.

He flung his senses out toward the small bridge. In his mind's eye he saw the rushing wall of water, watched it swallow the wooden planks and rip them free.

Shivering, he rubbed his upper arms. "It is done." Mason picked up his robe and turned toward the recessed doorway. It was time to go to Brianna.

*****

A roll of thunder jerked Brianna awake. She scrambled to her feet. Blinking, she looked around, for a moment lost as to where she was. With a quick inhale she remembered. As she spun toward the door it opened.

"Brianna." Mason stood in the doorway.

"I fell asleep."

He moved toward her.

Aftermath

"I–I'm sorry to pull you away from your guests," she stammered unnerved by his silence.

He stopped beside her and stared at the painting a long moment before turning to look into her eyes. "My guests are gone."

Brianna shifted, put a few more inches between them. "Well, I'm sure there's plenty of work left for me to do. I hope I didn't keep you from your bed." She hated how her words tumbled out, but she couldn't seem to stop their flow.

"You haven't." He looked away from her and toward the painting once again. Thunder rattled the windows. "It's raining."

"A little rain won't hurt me. I'll finish up and..."

"Brianna, it's four o'clock in the morning. The kitchen's fine. The catering staff left hours ago."

Four in the morning? It couldn't have been much past eleven when she'd found the room and the painting. She stepped back from him. "I don't understand. You must have known I wasn't in the kitchen."

"I knew where you were and that you were asleep."

"Why didn't you wake me?"

She started to turn, and he reached to touch her arm. "You can't go. I said it's raining."

"I've been wet before. I won't melt."

He ran a hand through his hair. "I'm not being clear. The rain caused a flash flood. My bridge is out. You can't leave."

She remembered the rush of water as she crossed the narrow bridge. "How long before they fix it?"

"At least morning, probably longer. The storm has downed power lines..."

"You still have lights," she said.

24

With a shrug, he said, "I have a generator. My home is self-sufficient and it's known. They won't be in a hurry."

"I've got to call..."

"The phone lines are down and who would you call?" he asked.

There it was again. Just how did this man know so much about her? It was true. There was no one she needed to call, but it irked her that he knew so she ignored his question. "I'll use my cell phone..."

"We are surrounded by trees. Mine doesn't work unless I hike to the top of..."

"How about some help instead of all the problems," she snapped.

He did not respond, but instead stared again at the painting."Now?" he whispered. He turned toward her. "It's time for us to cross."

Brianna frowned, and backed from him. "Say what?"

"Mirabella needs us."

Brianna shook her head, glanced toward the open door. "I don't know what you're talking about."

He reached out and clasped her shoulders. Where his hands touched her skin burned and she felt the heat flood through her.

"I...." The rest of her words died on her lips as she looked into his eyes. The room wavered and a roar filled her head. Her stomach dipped, rolled, and nausea rose into her throat as her vision grayed at the edges. Panicked, she grasped his forearms. "What's happening?"

His face blurred and then sharpened as he pulled her in close to his heart. "This time I will keep you safe, my Eleanor. Death will not part us again

too soon."

Who the hell was Eleanor? Her mind formed the question, demanded the answer, but before she could voice it oblivion claimed her.

Chapter Three

Brianna's Throat Burned and she gagged. Hands lifted her, settled into the middle of her back and held her up.

"Empty your stomach," a soft feminine voice ordered. "It will pass."

She fought to open her eyes.

"No, leave them closed for a moment more. There is a pail before you if needed."

She lost the battle with the choking nausea and let it come. Her body shook with the force of her retching.

"Will she be okay?" Mason Warren's voice asked from somewhere above her.

"She will be fine," the woman answered. "Sometimes the summoning warrants such reaction."

Brianna swallowed past the fire in her throat, but the sour taste in her mouth almost set her into another fit of vomiting

"Chew this."

Brianna felt a dry, hard disk placed in her hand.

"Ginger root. It will settle your stomach. Chew it now, child. " The voice held a no-nonsense warning.

Afraid to open her eyes Brianna lifted the disk to her nose and recognized the spicy scent. She put it into her mouth, chewed, and swallowed. It would take a few minutes. She'd used ginger root before for motion sickness, but she couldn't sit here with her eyes closed. She opened them.

The first thing she saw was an unlined face with the blush of youth in the cheeks. A cloud of golden hair haloed fair skin. Her gaze locked with eyes of purest blue. Instant recognition flashed through her muddled mind. "You?"

The woman drew back. "She's fully with us now."

"Can you sit up on your own?" Mason stood behind the woman and when Brianna nodded he circled to stand beside her. "Slide back against the pillow."

She did, but her gaze remained upon the woman. "Who are you?"

"I am Mirabella. Welcome to my home."

Her home? Brianna looked around the room. It was small, the walls a gray, muddy color. A fireplace, flames licking piled logs, took up a good part of the facing wall. A black round-bottomed pot hung from a hook above the flames. Dried herbs, tied in bundles, dangled from the ceiling's open beams. A table of dark wood stood in the middle of a brown-and-orange braided rug. Three chairs circled the table. Smaller braided rounds decorated their seats. A freestanding cupboard held a pewter bowl and pitcher.

Brianna licked her lips and fought to capture a coherent thought, but they refused to stop their panicked flutter inside her head. "I am not here," she managed to say.

Warm hands pried her death-grip from the coverings and held them gently. "Mirabella will explain," Mason said.

Her gaze locked on his face. "I'm at your house. I'm still asleep. You didn't come into the room and wake me."

"Let me, boy." Mirabella signaled Mason to release Brianna.

He stood.

The woman knelt beside the bed, placed her hands on Brianna's shoulders. "Listen to me, child."

Brianna swallowed, looked from the woman's face, toward Mason's, and back. It's a dream. It has to be.

"I am Mirabella and you are in Alamonar," the woman went on. "I wish there had been more time to prepare you, but the crossing had to be on Samhain. Even with Mason's help, my power could not bring you to me except this night when the curtain between your world and mine is the thinnest."

Brianna grabbed onto the only thing she comprehended of the woman's words. Samhain...the witch's new year. "Are you a witch?"

Mirabella smiled. "I am a sorceress."

"A sorceress. I see." Brianna's eyes shifted to Mason. "And you're a what...warlock?"

He frowned and looked away from her. "This isn't about me."

Let it all play out. It will make an interesting story when I wake up.

"Listen to me, Brianna Cole," the woman said. "I will tell you my tale and why I have brought you into my world."

When Brianna only stared, the sorceress went on.

"Alamonar balances upon a scale. A prophesized child will be born, sired by one Christian Samuels. Christian has no Power, but is heir to the magic of the Portents, and the child of his seed will tip the scale into good or into evil."

"I'm ready to wake up now," Brianna said, the beginnings of panic making her voice shake.

Mirabella held up a hand in warning. "You are not asleep, child. Just listen. I follow the Earth Goddess, Anete. I seek to heal the wounds of Alamonar, both past and present. Not so my craft sister, Katarina. She has chosen the black path to power. Her master, the dark god Rhonal, desires the homage of all who live in Alamonar. He whispers lies of wealth and immortality to those who will embrace him."

Brianna stared out the open door as more of the woman's words flowed over her.

"The foolish flock to his banner. There remain enough true to the Goddess to defy his reign, but the Child of Prophecy will tip the scales."

"I don't have any children," Brianna whispered.

Mirabella smiled. "You are not of my time. It is not for you to bear the child..."

"Then...?

"Heed the rest of my words." Mirabella's tone sharpened.

Brianna stood, gripped the side of the bed as her legs trembled. "I don't think I want to. I'm ready to go home now."

Mirabella placed both hands on Brianna's shoulders. "Child, you are in danger. It makes no difference which world you are in."

"What?"

She heard Mirabella sigh. "And for that I am responsible. I have turned Rhonal's eyes upon you. Will you hear the rest of my story?"

Brianna sank onto the edge of the cot and clasped her hands together. "Do I have a choice?"

She felt the measuring stare of the woman. "There are always choices."

The soft words made her heart pound. "Go ahead."

"You asked of the child. It is I the Goddess has chosen to bear Christian's son." A soft flush rose into Mirabella's cheeks. "In this lifetime Christian Samuels and I have been lovers for nine full moons, but we have loved each other in many forms and in many different lives.

"It is only this past fortnight I have been shown the Goddess' wishes. Christian knows of his place in the fate of Alamonar, but Katarina also is aware of the prophecy and Rhonal desires that she bear Christian's child. To this end she has taken my love prisoner." Mirabella's face paled to chalk-white and her lips thinned into a tight line before she said, "We will free him."

"We?" Brianna looked from Mason to Mirabella. "You can't mean me. I don't know anything about magic."

"Mason and I will free Christian. Your part is simple, you have but to give me a few drops of your blood, and remain alive until I have cast the spell."

"Remain alive?" Brianna parroted the words.

Mirabella reached into a pocket of her apron. She pulled out a smooth disc of white hanging from a braided cord. "I have charmed this amulet with wards of protection."

"Are you saying this Katarina wants me dead?"

Mirabella nodded. "She will stop at nothing to rule Alamonar."

Brianna went rigid with panic as Mirabella looped the cord over her head. Fear made her knees

shake, but she pressed them tightly together and asked, "And if I won't help you?"

Mirabella and Mason exchanged a quick look.

She stared into first one silent face and then the other. There's only their word I'm in another world. I'm probably in the woods, in Mason's backyard. If I can get away from them a short hike will take me to the road and then home. Maybe they're part of a weird vampire cult. Fine. Let them have their blood, then I am so out of here. She held out her arm. "You want a few drops," she emphasized a few, "then take them."

It was as if Mason read her mind. "You must not leave this glade," he said. "Katarina would have you before an hour went by."

She surged to her feet. "How do I know any of this is the truth?"

He stepped in front of her, but did not touch her.

Brianna went still. "Get out of my way."

"I helped to bring you here," he said. "I won't let Katarina have you."

"Why?" Brianna snapped. "I've got enough blood to go around."

"She does not require your blood," Mirabella said, "but she will make sure there is none for my use."

Brianna reached out blindly. Hands grabbed her shoulders and settled her back on the cot. "I want to go home," she said, and knew she sounded childish.

"And you will go home. I give you my word I will do all I can to protect you," Mirabella said. "Two days of your life and a few drops of blood. It is all I

require of you. There is no other. The Child of Prophecy must have Sarunos' blood flowing in his veins and you are the last of his line."

"But you said I couldn't have the child. And if I'm the last of his bloodline..."

Mirabella held up her hand. "The Goddess has given me the words to prepare a potion. Your blood is vital to it. Once I drink Sarunos will become part of me. In two sunsets there will be a solar eclipse. That is when I must prepare and drink the Goddess' magik."

Brianna licked her lips. "Just who is this Sarunos? And how the hell did I get his blood?"

"The name Sarunos Malachi means nothing to you?"

Brianna shook her head. "Was he a god here?"

"A mortal, but a mortal with strong powers of magik and even stronger beliefs of right and wrong." Mirabella sighed. "He made enemies, enemies who bargained with Rhonal to achieve their ends. Then, as now, Alamonar's fate rested upon a scale. The gods of light and dark battled, both evenly matched, and Sarunos was the prophesized child who would tip the balance.

"Rhonal sent those to tempt Sarunos with power, wealth and when he reached adulthood, women. But he chose the path of light, tipped the scales to justice and right, and Alamonar prospered." She paused to smile. "Rhonal was shunned, almost forgotten in time. And does a god exist if it is not worshipped? Rhonal began to doubt his own existence, seethed and fumed, survived only on his hatred for Sarunos. Continually he

whispered his black promises to evil hearts." Mirabella stared down at Brianna.

"Rhonal formed a plan to murder Sarunos before he could father a child and continue his line.

"Lilith was Sarunos' love. They married and ruled Alamonar with wisdom. But she did not conceive, and at night, as she dreamed, Rhonal whispered lies into her heart. Lilith's handmaiden, Evangeline, fell beneath the dark god's influence. She told Lilith of a witch-woman whose spells would make her womb fertile and late one eve, Evangeline led Lilith from the palace." Mirabella moved away, turned her back to Brianna.

"The witch-woman, in truth Rhonal himself, told Lilith her barren condition was not her fault, but her husband's. He gave her a potion to awaken her husband's seed. The next eve Lilith offered her husband a goblet of wine, in the morning he lay dead."

"Oh, my God," Brianna said. "But then how...?"

"That is the irony, Lilith was already with child. Knowing the truth too late she fled the castle." Mirabella touched Brianna's shoulder. "My great-great grandfather's grandfather sent her into your world to hide, and Sarunos' line continued.

"On into me," Brianna said, still not sure she believed any of it.

Mirabella nodded. "You are the last. Rhonal's hate has festered and now, with the coming of the prophesied child, it has burst."

Mason put his hand on Brianna's arm. "You won't be safe in either world until the child's conceived."

Brianna raised her head. "And he'd kill me to stop you from using my blood?"

"Rhonal will not kill you, the other god and goddesses will not permit it, but they will not stay the hearts and hands of those who obey his wishes," Mirabella said.

"When I agreed to help Mirabella, I did not know it was you, but I swore I would protect the last of Sarunos' bloodline," Mason's lips thinned, "and this time I will. You must trust me."

This time? What did he mean? And there's something else, he said it right before I passed out. What was it? But it wouldn't come to her and Brianna pushed the thought away. She just couldn't handle anything more right now. "Trust you? Now why would I do that? I'll keep myself safe, thank you very much."

His jaw tensed, but he turned away in silence.

"Will you help?" Mirabella said, as she moved to stand near the cot.

Brianna closed her eyes for a moment and then opened them and said. "I have to. If I want my life back."

"I am sorry, but such is the truth of it," Mirabella said. "With a night's rest I could return you, but you will remain in danger for the rest of your life. And if you have children of your own, they too will be in danger from Rhonal. Without Sarunos' blood the Child of Prophecy will lead Alamonar into darkness. An evil that will spread..."

"I get it," Brianna said. "I said I'd stay."

"Thank you. All of Alamonar is in your debt." Mirabella turned and walked toward the cottage door.

"Hey, where are you going," Brianna asked.

"I must fast and commune with the Goddess Anete."

"But what do I do?" Brianna didn't want the other woman to leave her here, alone with Mason.

"Heed Mason's words. He will keep you safe."

Brianna glared at Mason and she heard Mirabella sigh. "Child, when I saw who you were and that this time you were a woman of mature years and not a mere girl I rejoiced. Do not prove my relief wrong. Listen to Mason's words. He knows what we face and has my complete trust. You are of the most importance to me. Do you think I would take a chance with your fate? I will return soon." Mirabella walked out the cottage door.

In the brush, well away from the warded cottage, a fox watched the sorceress leave. Its yellow eyes turned once again to the door, ears flicked forward. Should he stay and watch or return to his mistress with news the one had arrived?

The cottage door remained closed.

With a flick of his tail he turned and darted into the darkness of the trees.

Chapter Four

The Hearth's Flames danced on the pile of logs. Katarina gloried in the waves of warmth that caressed her naked form. She lifted her hands and combed her fingers through her mane of curls. Today she had chosen a molten scarlet hue for her tresses, much the same color as the blood she yearned to watch flow from Mirabella's scrawny neck. The vibrant strands were like silk twining around her fingers. She could have tamed them into a subdued braid with a single word, but instead enjoyed the softness of their kiss upon her bare shoulders and hips.

Without turning she knew exactly when Vulpine arrived. She closed her eyes, felt his lust overflow, and her nipples tightened in response. Perhaps this eve she would shape-change into a vixen and couple with him beneath the stars. A smile curved her lips, but was erased before she faced him.

Vulpine shifted back into human form and dropped to his knees before her. She stared for a moment at his bowed head. With his broad shoulders and narrow hips he was easy enough on the eyes. His fingers were long and slim and knew how to pleasure a woman's body. A pity he was not the one she craved. "Vulpine, rise."

"Mistress."

Katarina let his gaze devour her face a moment before she lifted an eyebrow in warning.

"The blood heir of Sarunos is here," Vulpine

said, lowering his gaze.

"Male or female?"

"Female."

Damnation. A man would have been more pleasant to subdue. She waited in silence for him to continue.

"Brianna, she is called. There is another with her, a man. I feel a power within him, but it is blocked."

Katarina waved a hand in dismissal. "Then he is not a threat to me. It is the woman I want."

She whirled to walk back to the fireplace and stared into the flames. "Mirabella has made her last mistake. She thinks she does as her vapid earth goddess wills, but Rhonal leads her like a leashed pet down his path."

"The dark god, he you serve..."

Katarina spun to face him. "I serve no one." Her icy tone emphasized the word 'serve.' "We have an alliance that profits both. I give to him this woman who has the blood of Sarunos in her veins and he will give to me the Child of Prophecy. With the infant comes Christian and all of Alamonar."

"Mistress, please, a question?"

She nodded her head, willing to indulge him a moment longer.

"Why does the Dark God wish the Heir of the Ancients?"

Katarina shrugged. "All I have been told is those with the blood of Sarunos must die. And this, Brianna, is the last. Enough questions. Help me dress. It is time for a visit to my guest." She watched his face flush and smiled. "What gown will it be this day? Perhaps the forest green? Or the sky blue? Which will bring Christian to his knees before

me?"

Katarina knew it enraged Vulpine to help in her plan of Christian's seduction. She watched his eyes narrow to slits. He despised her games and had urged her to force an appeasement elixir between the man's lips and order him to lie with her. Perhaps he was right, no, she wanted Christian to love her of his free will and he would. How could he not? No man refused her.

She turned from him and moved to a freestanding wardrobe. Katarina whispered an incantation and felt her hair rise from her body. It separated into three plaits and braided itself into one long rope. When she felt its weight fall softly to graze her waist she turned, satisfaction soothed her as she saw the yearning upon Vulpine's face. She smiled and lifted her hands above her head in a languid stretch. Yes, Christian would come to her; it was only a matter of time. The smile faded. But time was against her. She would give her reluctant lover-to-be one more day. Then they would lay together, one way or the other.

Katarina reached into the wardrobe and pulled a sky-blue gown free. She lifted it above her head and let its softness flow down her body. The translucent gown teased with beckoning shadows. The neckline dipped into a deep V that just covered her peach-hued nipples. She took a step forward and a slit in the skirt, all the way to her waistline, opened and showed a flash of bare skin.

Vulpine groaned.

With a satisfied smile, she turned her back to him. "Do my laces." She heard him move to her, felt his fingers caress the middle of her back before he drew the first laces together. A fire ignited in her

lower stomach. She thrust her buttocks back against him and found the evidence of his desire. Vulpine's hands stilled and, with a throaty laugh, she dipped her knees and then straightened, rubbing herself against his length.

His breath came, hot against the back of her neck, and she felt his hands slide into the sides of the gown. His fingers slipped along her skin, traveled upward. She waited until they reached the curves of her breasts, and then pulled away. "The laces," she said coldly. "My guest awaits."

His fingers hesitated for a moment, trembled, and then returned to her back and the laces of her gown.

Yes, tonight she would reward him with a frolic among the trees.

Chapter Five

Mason Watched Brianna wander the room. Her restless gaze lighted upon everything but him. When he could take no more he moved to block her path. "Are you ready to listen?"

She frowned at him a moment and then nodded.

"I'm a witch in our world." He watched her face for her reaction. Otherwise he would have missed her quick suppression of fear. It didn't surprise him. "Brianna, do you believe in reincarnation?"

She did not answer right away, just stared beyond his shoulder. "What does that have to do with right now?"

"This is my fifth life," Mason said. "And in each I have been born a witch." But you know this, he silently added. You have been a part of each of them.

Brianna frowned. "You remember lives before?"

"You don't?"

"I didn't say I believed in such stuff."

"But you do." It wasn't a question. Whether she admitted it or not some part of her believed.

"I've had dreams. Bits and pieces are clear," she said with a shrug.

He was surprised at her words. Even now, her strength pulsed between them. As she'd lain on the cot, he'd stared into her face and remembered their previous times together. Did he dare tell her? "Have you opened yourself to the past?"

41

"What's the point?" She gave him a hard look. "Did you know of Sarunos Malachi?

He nodded. "Yes. I've known Mirabella and Alamonar from before. She required my help."

"And mine?" She rubbed her upper arms.

"You're cold."

Her lips curved into a slight smile. "I'm not sure what I am."

His own long yawn caught him by surprise.

"Have you slept at all?" she said.

His answer was a short shake of his head.

She pointed to the cot. "Go ahead."

"I have to watch..."

"I promise to be a good girl." When he still hesitated, she added. "I'm not stupid, you know."

His face flushed. "I never thought you were."

"Then show a little trust." She held his gaze until he looked away.

"Fine." He moved to the cot. "If anything...and I mean anything seems odd, wake me."

"I'll scream loud enough to drag Sarunos himself from his grave, moldy bones and all."

Stretched out upon the cot, he looked at her. "Do not remove the amulet." His eyes closed.

*****

"Is it okay if I go outside?"

When Mason did not answer, Brianna crossed to the cot and looked down at him. Most of the tense lines had left his face. With a small smile, she drew a soft quilt up the length his body. Her fingers grazed his hip and he moaned softly. At the sound, embers sprang into existence in her lower stomach. She stepped back and stared down at him. Whoa. It's been awhile, but I know a sexual ping when I feel it. What gives? He's not my type. She liked her

men with a little more bulk, and he looked underfed.

Mason's hair had escaped its band and lay in a black curtain against his shoulder. She watched the rise and fall of his chest for a moment before reaching out to touch a strand. It was warm from his body and soft beneath her fingers. His lips parted and released a soft snore. Brianna drew her hand back with a smile. He had a wonderful mouth, sensual, but not feminine. She'd found herself watching his lips whenever he spoke, but it was his eyes, the smoky blue of a summer sky right before sun set, that blazed his feelings. He'd never make a good poker player.

She moved her gaze over him. He'd spent some time outdoors, his bronze skin told her so and he had to have some Native American blood flowing through him with that hair and chiseled cheekbones. Her fingers hesitated above his lips, and a memory floated through her mind of him trembling at her touch, his eyes darkening to cobalt-blue. They'd been together before, he a witch like he'd said, and she a warrior priestess.

Mason groaned and she could see the hard outline of his arousal tent the black robe he wore. Is he dreaming about me? The thought made her breath quicken. If I join him...? Her nipples hardened and the embers of heat in her stomach flared into full flame, flowed downward and pooled between her thighs. The cottage seemed to stifle and grow smaller by the second.

"My God, I need a cold shower," she whispered. "What the hell. He didn't say I couldn't go out, just to be careful."

Outside, she lifted her scorched cheeks to a cool wind. 'Do you believe in reincarnation, Mason

43

had asked.

She closed her eyes and a scene played out in the darkness behind them.

A richly dressed man, raven haired and brown eyed, her husband Victor, kneeling beside an ornate bed, a woman, Eleanor, herself, lying inside it.

His words as she'd passed out, 'I won't let you die too soon this time, my Eleanor.' Goosebumps formed on her arms, but she did not open her eyes. She had to know.

The woman's face was pale and strained. The small hand lying in his trembled.

"Don't leave me, my love," he begged. "The mid-wife comes."

The woman, Eleanor, gasped as another pain ripped through her.

Brianna knew something was wrong. So wrong.

A maid came hurrying into the room with a armful of clean cloths. She moved the covering aside. "She still bleeds, my Lord. I cannot stop it."

"And the babe?"

"Your son is fine, my Lord."

Eleanor's body shuddered. "Victor," she whispered. "Our son thrives."

"As will his mother," he said and brought her hand to his lips.

She smiled. "I will always love you. Care for our son."

"No, Eleanor. No..."

Brianna opened her eyes. Her cheeks were wet with tears. She looked toward the cottage door. "Victor," she whispered, and knew it was the first life they'd shared together.

She stood and walked to a well. Staring down

into its black depths she hugged her stomach.

Scenes of their three other lives streaked through her mind. In each he had tried to protect her, and in each she had died, too soon.

A soft whine reached her ears. She held her breath and listened. It came from beneath a bush. She moved toward it.

Inside the thick brush's spiked leaves she saw only shadows. Had she'd imagined the sound? But the whine came again, full of fear. Brianna saw a flash of golden eyes. "Come here. I'm not going to hurt you." She didn't relish the thought of sticking her hand beneath the brush. She knew she'd at least get scratched for her efforts and possibly bitten.

Brianna sat back on her heels and looked around. "You've got to come out." Her answer was a soft growl. Maybe she'd find something in the cottage to lure it from the brush?

In a cupboard, she discovered a wedge of soft white cheese. She broke off a chunk and hurried back to the bush. "Look what I've got," she said, and waved the cheese in front of a branch.

She heard another soft whine. "Come on. It's for you, but you've got to come out."

"Brianna?"

The sharp word made her jump. "Quiet. You'll scare it," she said, glancing over her shoulder at Mason.

"Please stand back."

His shadow fell across her and she looked up. He held an ax.

"Just what do you plan to do with that?"

Mason glared down at her and she heard the tenseness in his voice as he spoke. "Have you forgotten Mirabella's words?"

"We're still inside her magic protection."

A frown creased his forehead. "Katarina has magic also."

A whine came from beneath the bush. "Listen. It's some kind of animal. It's scared, maybe even hurt."

"And possibly sent here by Katarina. Its claws could be poisoned."

Brianna waved her hand at him. "Quiet. It's coming out."

Mason pushed her to the side and she sprawled full length upon the wet grass. "What the hell?" she sputtered, as she scrambled to her knees.

He waved the ax at her in clear warning.

"Wait," she urged. "If it's harmless it'll cost you nothing but a few minutes. If not...."

A black-tipped snout emerged from the brush. It sniffed the air and a small, shaggy, gray head appeared. Golden eyes looked from her to Mason while white-edged ears flicked like twin radars.

"It's a puppy," Brianna said.

"A wolf," Mason said and raised the ax.

She grabbed his arm. "What do you think you're doing?"

The pup growled and bared its teeth.

"You're scaring it," she said.

Mason looked around. "Just where is its mother?"

"Perhaps killed with an ax," she said, her voice sharp with sarcasm. She tossed a piece of the cheese in front of the pup. It looked from her, then to Mason and then lunged forward and grabbed the cheese.

"It doesn't look dangerous," Brianna said. "If

you're afraid something's wrong then check it out. You're a witch too."

His cheeks flushed. "I can't."

Her eyes narrowed. "What do you mean you can't?

"My magic doesn't work here," he muttered. "I'm not of this time."

She tossed the pup another piece of cheese. "I'm not going to stand here and watch you hack it to death."

He glared at her. "Then go back inside the cottage."

"I don't think so."

"Brianna." His voice rose.

"What's going on here?" The words came from behind them and they turned. Mirabella stood there.

Brianna crossed her arms over her breasts. "It's a wolf pup."

"It may have been sent by Katarina," Mason said.

"But he doesn't know," Brianna said. "Not for sure."

Mirabella stretched her arms out toward the pup, palms up. "I don't sense any taint of Katarina's magic."

Mason stared hard at the wolf. "I suppose I could take it deep into the forest..."

"It's too young. It will die all by itself," Brianna said. "Can't you tell if it has bad magic?"

Mirabella frowned. "I can, but..."

Brianna touched the woman's arm. "Please."

Mirabella sighed, then closed her eyes and began to chant. The words were low and melodious, their cadence a soft rise and fall of sound. Mirabella opened her eyes. "There is no magic in the wolf

pup."

Brianna smiled. "Then I can touch it?"

"If she will let you." Mirabella inclined her head.

"She?"

"It's a girl. I felt her story as I searched. Gnawer, she is, was, called by her mother. Her mother is dead, her neck snapped by a trap."

The pup stood and walked toward Brianna.

"She has decided to claim you as her new pack."

Brianna dropped to her knees beside the pup and scratched between its ears. "I'll take care of you little Gnawer."

"Child?" Mirabella said. "What about when you return to your time? What of Gnawer then?"

"Can you send her with me?" The words were out before Brianna realized she'd said them.

"I can, but will she be accepted in your town?"

Brianna looked at the pup. Gnawer would pass for a German Sheppard, but she wasn't allowed a dog in her place.

"She could stay with me," Mason said.

Brianna stared at him. "Thank you, but just until I find a new place to live." She pointed. "Gnaw, this is Mason. Mason, Gnaw."

He held out his hand to the pup. She took two steps and stretched her neck forward to sniff his fingers. She whined and then rolled over and presented her stomach.

"You two are Gnaw's new parents." Mirabella motioned toward the cottage door. "Now, may I suggest we return inside?"

"Why are you back?" Mason asked as they walked toward the door.

"The Goddess requires something more from me." She glanced from Mason to Brianna. "It seems my return was a good thing, bless the Goddess."

Brianna reached to pet the wolf's head. "It was for Gnaw."

"To show caution was justified," Mirabella said.

At the doorway Mason stepped to the side and allowed the women to enter first.

Mirabella crossed the room, pried a stone free of the wall and reached inside. When she pulled her hand back she held a small leather bag. She opened the bag, poured three colored stones into her palm, then replaced it and tapped the rock back into place. She turned, saw Brianna's look, and held them out toward her. "Spell stones, a gift from the Goddess. I use them to focus my power."

They looked like polished agates, clear with swirls of brown and gold.

Mirabella held up the smallest of the three. "This one I found inside a hen's egg." She smiled. "I see the doubt on your face and accept it. If there were more time..." Her words trailed off.

"What about the other two?"

Mirabella picked up the largest stone. "This one I've had since I first discovered my power. I was three years old. I woke to find it resting against my heart. As I touched it the Goddess spoke her words to me. It was the first to go into my soul-essence bag."

"That's the bag...."

Mirabella nodded. "Inside it is all that makes me want I am."

"And the third?"

Mirabella's cheeks tinged with pink. "I birthed

the stone following the first time Christian and I were together in this life." She closed her hand over them and turned toward the door. "I will not return until the time of the casting is upon us. All will be well?"

Brianna glanced at Mason. "Everything will be Fine, I'll just fix Gnaw a bed and find her something to eat."

"Good. Then I will say farewell for now." Mirabella walked out the cottage door and shut it behind her.

A stilted quiet reigned. Brianna dared a look at Mason and saw him comb his fingers through his hair. He moved toward the cottage door. "Where are you going?"

"I'll be within hearing range."

Understanding dawned. There must be a privy out back.

"Don't worry about us." Brianna patted Gnaw's head. "We'll be fine."

Mason replied by walking out the door.

"Let's get you something to eat," Brianna said.

A quick exploration of the cottage netted some dried meat and berries to go with the earlier discovered cheese. She mixed it all together in a bowl and added water to soften. "Here you go."

Gnaw sniffed it, gave Brianna a doubtful look and then took a small bite. With a little warble of pleasure she lay before the bowl and with her paws cradling it, went to eating with gusto.

Brianna laughed. She filled another bowl with water and while the pup ate found a blanket, folded it and placed it in a corner out of the way.

She glanced toward the door. Mason had been

gone awhile. How long could it take to pee? She tried to ignore the unease that twitched along the back of her neck.

Gnaw crossed to lick Brianna's hand and then went to inspect her new bed. It must have met her standards, for she settled down and closed her eyes.

Brianna touched the bone disc around her neck. It protected her, but what about Mason? She walked to the door and looked out. "I'm sure he's okay." But it wouldn't hurt to take a quick look. Her hand clutching the talisman, she walked toward the back.

A garden took up a large part of the area behind the cottage. She could see squash vines, ablaze with orange blossoms. More vines crawled up poles. Green beans dangled in clusters from them. Corn stalks, their heads tasseled with gold, stood in straight lines like soldiers in a dress parade. Red tomatoes peeked from still more mounds of green. A garish scarecrow flapped his arms in a sudden breeze and startled her for a moment, but then she smiled as she walked by.

She and the scarecrow were the only ones in the garden. No sign of a privy. Maybe they used the great outdoors here. Brianna hoped not.

She'd turned back toward the cottage when she heard it, a tuneless humming. The sound came from behind a curtain of blooming star jasmine.

The humming changed to words. "Puff the magic dragon..." Mason screeched out.

The man could not sing. If she hadn't known the words to the old song she would never have recognized it. Brianna grinned and with a good-natured ribbing comment in mind, she walked

to the vine curtain. Ready to fling her jest, she pushed a cluster of white flowers aside.

The teasing words stuck in her throat.

Sun filtered through trees and dappled the pond. Mason stood waist deep in the pool of clear water, his back toward her. Wet hair hugged his head and hung halfway down his well-muscled form. He took a step toward the far bank and the water receded, showed her a white tan line. He took another step.

He's getting out. I shouldn't be standing here. But Brianna couldn't make her feet move.

Mason's buttocks were white and taunt, the muscles tensing and releasing with each forward motion.

Brianna drew harsh gulps of air into her lungs.

On the bank, Mason bent to pick up his robe and she moaned.

He stiffened and whipped around.

Their gazes locked.

Brianna felt heat suffuse her and she stepped forward.

Mason made no attempt to cover his body.

She broke eye contact and let her gaze roam across his chest and downward. Sleek and jutting, his arousal was clear. He wanted her as much as she wanted him.

"I remembered," she said and moved toward him.

He dropped his robe as she neared. She stopped in front of him and without words he reached to untie the drawstring of her peasant blouse. He pushed the blouse from her shoulders. The soft cotton slid down her skin and caught on the swell of her breasts. His fingertips grazed her back

as he unclasped her strapless bra, and she moaned as it slid downward. The moan became a gasp as his warm lips touched her flesh and moved across her collarbone. She felt her nipples harden. Mason lifted his head, and she read the question within his gaze. She cradled his cheeks with her palms and drew his mouth toward hers.

His body was different this time, taller and thinner, but the emotions that flared as their lips touched rang true. She curled her fingers into his wet hair and let the feelings sweep over her.

Need surged, hot and welcome, it had been so damn long. Mason tore his mouth from hers. She heard his ragged exhale and thrilled at the sound. Holding her gaze with his, she ran her hands over his chest and watched his face flush as she gave a little sigh of approval. She explored lower and felt his stomach muscles quiver.

With a groan, Mason grabbed her hand and raised it to his lips. "I've known your body in many lives. In each I've ached to touch you, and it is always like the first time." His fingers traced a ribbon of fire up her spine. "I've wondered what you were like beneath that skirt and blouse."

She tried to speak, but it was if the air had evaporated. Instead, she tugged at the elastic waistband of her skirt.

"Let me," he said, and she felt his fingers at her waist. Brianna gasped as he pushed the full skirt down the length of her legs. When it was bunched around her feet, he lifted her and she kicked it away. He set her down and stepped back. She stood in nothing but satiny, white bikini panties.

His gaze swept over her. "I've always loved undressing you, enjoyed the sight as each article fell from your body. But I must say I do like those

panties."

She laughed. "Maybe I should just leave them on."

His answer was to hook his fingers in the panties' elastic band and skim them down her legs. "No, I like you best like this."

A breeze stirred, danced across her naked skin.

He held out his arms to her, and she stepped into him. His teeth raked across her shoulder, and she felt him bury his face in her hair. He ran his hands down her body, across her hips, and up her flat stomach to cup her breasts. She felt his greed, and her own rose to match it. She looped her hands around his neck and leaned back, offering. His hand slid down, pressed between her legs and she felt herself plunge toward the jagged edge of release. "My God."

"It's been so long. I want to be inside you," he whispered into her neck. Her knees buckled, and he followed her down. Stretched out upon the grass, he rose on his elbows and looked again into her eyes. "You are mine, for now and always."

Her blood raged, and she reached for him. He was hot and hard in her grasp. "Now," she said, as she urged him toward her. She wrapped her legs around him and he slid slowly in—slid deeper when she lifted her hips to meet him. Held there, with her breath trapped in her throat, she became lost in a haze of pleasure.

"Look at me. See what you do to me?" Mason demanded. She stared upward into a face, tight with restraint

Their gazes locked, and they began to move, at first almost lazily, and she wallowed in the

pleasure. Then it wasn't enough, and the beat quickened, flesh glided over flesh. She felt him tense, and he thrust into her with a hoarse cry. His shudders triggered hers and sent her flying into release.

Chapter Six

Katarina Stood Before the closed door. She inhaled deeply, smoothed her gown, frowned when she saw that her fingers trembled. He is but a man, she reminded herself in exasperation.

Behind her, Vulpine stirred. "Leave us,' she said, without turning.

His quick intake of breath filled her ears, followed by the sharp slap of his heels on stone as he moved away.

Katarina pressed her fingers against her fluttering stomach and then lifted them to trace a pattern upon the face of the door. She pushed it inward.

He stood before the window, stared out. An untouched tray, with this morn's food to break the fast, stood upon an ornate table of gold and polished metal.

She frowned. In the three days he had been here he had eaten nothing.

"Good eve, Christian," she said and moved toward him.

He did not turn.

"Perhaps you would like a stroll in the garden?"

"You wish to walk your pet? Why do you not just put a collar on me? Ah, but then you have, a collar--magic." His voice was harsh with bitterness.

She knew he referred to the wards that surrounded the windows and doors. She'd warned him not to attempt escape. Of course he did not listen and had tried. It surprised her she did not find

joy in his pain as he had writhed upon the floor. "My only wish is to see my love happy."

His body stiffened, and he turned. His golden gaze flicked over her. She devoured him with her eyes, took in his broad shoulders and narrow hips. His pale blonde hair had drifted forward to frame an eye and he pushed it back with an irritated murmur. By-the-Dark-God, he stole her breath. She wanted those hands upon her, those fingers inside her. She could taste his tongue, feel it upon her nipples. She groaned and pressed her legs together.

He laughed and her face grew hot.

"I do not care for a stroll around my prison. Thank you very much."

Irritated, she moved to stand between him and the window and let the late sun highlight the shadow of her body. His gaze moved over her, paused at her breasts, and she felt her nipples harden. Oh, yes. You will be mine, Christian Samuels. His pupils enlarged and her breath came fast.

Then a cold smile twisted his lips and he stepped around her and stared again out the window.

Cold shock gripped her heart—and then fiery rage. A killing incantation formed in her head and she pointed a trembling finger at him.

"*Cease.*" The word flared inside her mind, singed her blood and she pressed her hands to the sides of her head and moaned.

"I'm sorry. Release me."

The dark voice in her head went on. "*Once I have the child, then you may do what you wish, but until then he will live.*"

"I understand, my Lord."

"No. I think you do not. I tire of these games. The man will not come willingly to you. Say what is needed."

"But, Lord?"

"It is my command.

"Yes. Lord." The pain ceased and she turned to meet Christian's hot, glaring eyes.

"Rhonal tightening the.chain?"

"Just a reminder of the glory to come." She came closer to him. "Christian, I have been patient, but I will have your seed. It will be my body the Child of Prophecy grows within and not that of the bitch Mirabella."

"Do not speak her name with your filthy lips." Anger turned his cheeks dull red.

Of course, why hadn't she seen it earlier? Because she'd been so sure she could get him to submit to her. No man had ever refused her.

"Your precious Mirabella." She held out her open hand. A rose blossomed inside of it "I hold her life." Staring into his eyes, she clenched her hand into a fist. When she opened it, the rose had been reduced to black cinders. She blew into her hand, the cinders disappeared. "What will you do to save her?" She watched the blood leave his face and smiled.

"Mirabella serves the Goddess Anete...I serve the Goddess Anete. We are not without power. And with the coming of the one with the blood of Sarunos..."

"The Goddess." Katarina laughed. "Her power is that of a lamp to the sun where my dark lord is concerned. As to the other, she has already been seen to." Katarina reached to caress his cheek. He went rigid at her touch. "Mirabella will never carry

the child, but we will let her live, her and many others." She ran her fingers down his chest. "The choice is yours."

"At what cost?" he whispered.

"You are the price..."

"My seed..."

"Willingly given and not just for one night, but until I tire of you. We will rule Alamonar...." Her words faded at his look of pity.

"I will never love you, Katarina."

"Never is a long time, Christian." She took a step back from him. "What is it to be?"

He frowned. "You wish an answer at this moment?"

"I have waited long enough."

"If I pleasure you with my body, all will live?" he said.

Katarina shook her head. "Not all, but some. Rhonal will have the woman who has the taint of Sarunos inside her. I will have you, and Mirabella will have life."

"Then Mirabella has done so?" Hope filled his voice. "Brought the one of Sarunos' bloodline from the other world."

Katarina laughed. "Yes. The fool has brought her almost to our stoop."

"Her? What will Rhonal do with...?"

"It is of no concern to you," Katarina said. "Which will it be? Does Mirabella live or...?"

"What if I cannot perform?"

She reached out, stroked the length of him and felt him quiver beneath her touch. "I doubt it will be problem."

"You've bewitched me," Christian snapped

and twisted away from her.

Katarina shrugged. "Believe what you wish."

"My body may service you, but that will be all."

For now, she thought, but you will come to love me.

Christian reached to loosen the drawstring at his trousers. "So be it."

"No," she was surprised to hear her herself say. "It will be tonight. I wish to prepare myself for you."

He smiled bitterly. "What special plans do you need for a rutting?"

She turned from him. "Tonight, Christian. It is what I wish." With her anger in check, she moved toward the chamber door. Before she exited, she looked back. He stared out the window once more.

Doubt and unease pricked her. What if she could not make him love her? Then she would enjoy his body and be content with the fact he was hers, and not the whore Mirabella's.

She moved down the hall, stopped before an ornate mirror. "Of course he will love me," she said to her reflection. "How can he not?"

A door opened and Vulpine came into the hall. She beckoned toward him."Would you care to walk with me in the garden?"

He looked taken back at her question, but then hurried toward her. She smiled at the eager hotness in his gaze. Yes. One must always reward a faithful servant. She took his arm and let him lead her toward the door

Aftermath

*****

Katarina stretched and smiled. Beside her on the bed of columbine, the white blossoms still fresh and warmed by her magic, Vulpine slept in exhaustion. She looked at the furrows of still flowing blood that striped his back and felt an ember of lust flare. By-the-Dark-God, they had ridden hard and fast and he had given as much as he'd taken.

Vulpine turned upon his back and her gaze strayed to his flaccid member. So innocent it looked, but she knew with but a touch it would be standing and ready again for action. She toyed with the idea and then sighed; there was much to do before this day ended. With a scarlet-coated fingernail, she flicked his nipple. "Vulpine. Wake. I have need of you."

He stretched and, with eyes still closed, smiled and reached out for her.

Katarina slapped his hands away. "Awake, I say."

His eyes flew open and, for an unguarded moment stared, full of hate, into hers. The glint of unleashed anger, although quickly shielded, did what all of the shape-changer's fawning jealousy could not—made her lust leap.

What difference could a few more minutes make, she thought, as she rose onto her knees and straddled him.

*****

Vulpine again in fox form, wove among the trees. Behind him, the two-footers, crashed and stomped, and with each noise his ire rose. He wanted to turn and dig his fangs into them, but Katarina's orders were clear. Their bodies were needed to break the wards around Mirabella's

61

cottage. He hoped he had brought enough. With each incineration, the witch-woman's magic would weaken, until he would be able to walk through the wards unharmed; at least that was what Katarina had promised. She had surmised ten deaths would do, and to that end he now led fourteen stumbling buffoons. If the wards do not kill the most of them I will, he thought, as he heard a loud curse rise from behind yet again.

He halted and let the group surround him. It was time for a little fun. He stepped into their center and closed his eyes, willing the change to begin. Groans of fear filled his ears and he smelled its acrid taint. What did they see, he wondered? He had never seen the change, his eyes had to remain closed for the complete concentration it required. Once it had been described to him...the fog that oozed from his fur or skin, depending upon if he was becoming the fox or returning to his human form. How it formed an opaque shroud that obscured him from sight, how his bones snapped and cracked, and a scent like a recent lightning strike radiated from within.

Vulpine knew from the feel of his body the change was complete. He opened his eyes. He stood naked before them. White faces ringed him. Only a few stout souls, five of them, did not tremble like wind-whipped saplings. Their stoic attitudes irritated him so he singled them out first.

"Go through the trees and to the door, but you must all enter the clearing at the same time." It would not do for them to see what befell the one who went first. They were be-spelled by Katarina to obey his words, so they nodded and turned from him. The other nine started to follow and he froze

them in place with a single look. "I did not give you leave to move."

The screams came to them first, and then the smell, charred flesh. He watched the faces of the nine before him. They paled, and a wild fear entered their eyes, a panic so feral that one broke free from Katarina's spell and turned to run. "Stop him."

And the eight fell upon the ninth with fists, feet, and teeth. He watched with detachment until he judged the man no longer a problem. "Enough."

They stepped back. The bloody mess before him already attracted flies. Katarina would not be happy with the waste. But the remaining eight would be enough to fulfill her wishes.

"Follow me."

They moved to the glade. The eight stopped at the sight of the five charred bodies. Smoke still rose from them. He heard gagging and then retching from those behind him. He smelled their fear, and it was a tribute to Katarina's control the eight still moved into the glade.

Vulpine stopped before the door of the cottage. Now that the wards were gone, he could open himself up to Katarina. He felt when she touched his mind.

"No one is within," she said. *"They are out back."*

He nodded and turned to glare into each set of eyes. They'd been instructed not to speak, to only follow his lead, and then fall upon any he pointed to. They were not to hurt the girl, but the man was fair game. He only wished he could stay behind and join in the fun, but his orders had been clear. He was to return at once with her.

Vulpine led them around the cottage. Across a

garden patch, he heard soft voices. He stopped, cocked his head, and listened as he sniffed the air. The rich smell of sex filled his nose. He turned to those behind him and waved them forth with his head. The wind shifted, and he caught the scent of something else, wild and feral—a wolf. Where did the scent come from? His answer came—a chorus of furious barking. He whirled to face the corner of the cottage. A wolf pup charged around it, still in full voice. From the trees beyond, alarmed voices rose. "Go," he shouted to the eight. "Do as was commanded by your mistress." His anger surged at the unplanned occurrence. The pup would die for its interference. He turned to face it and snarled. He expected the pup to stop, but instead it swerved by him and continued to run. For an instant, surprise kept him rooted in place, and then he gave chase.

Vulpine charged from the trees, almost running full force into the pool of water, before he swerved at the last moment.

The man and woman were both naked. She stood behind the man, holding the wolf pup in her arms. The eight ringed them. The man was in fighting stance. This was not the plan. They were to have fallen upon him unaware. The eight looked at him for guidance. The man guarded the woman. That was the key. She pressed close to the man, and the wolf pup in her arms growled as she spoke to it.

"Easy, Gnaw." Her voice rang loud and strong. "Easy."

"What do you want?" the man demanded.

"Katarina wishes to speak to the woman."

Vulpine watched her shake her head.

"I don't think so," she said.

"You heard Brianna's answer," the man said,

his hands held away from his sides.

"Katarina feels the woman should hear her offer. Does Mirabella fear her words may not be found true?"

The man flushed. "Mirabella does not lie." He took a step toward Vulpine and the eight shifted, tightened their circle.

"No, Mason," the woman said.

Vulpine motioned toward the eight men. "They have no will but Katarina's. I've but to give the command and you will die."

The man laughed. "You won't do that. Your mistress wants Brianna."

"She does," Vulpine agreed. "But she does not want you."

The woman gasped. "She just wants to talk to me, right?"

Vulpine nodded.

"Brianna, don't be a fool," the man muttered. "You heard what Mirabella said."

Brianna stared straight at Vulpine. "If I go with you, no one will be hurt?"

"My orders where to bring you. How it was to be done was left to me."

She held out the pup to the man. "Take Gnaw."

"No, Brianna."

"Can you beat them all?" She looked at him, her face concerned.

"I can try."

"And you can die." She touched his arm. "Then who will come to get me if you are dead?"

He took the pup from her.

"A wise move friend," Vulpine goaded.

Anger tightened the man's lips. He gathered

65

the pup to his chest as it whined in distress at leaving the woman's arms. "I'll come for you."

"Of course you will." She stepped around the man.

At a look from Vulpine, the eight parted the circle. She walked through, and the circle again closed.

He reached to take her arm, and she jerked away from him. "I need my clothes."

"Get them," he ordered. "And bring me his."

Silence stretched as they both dressed. He turned to her and offered his arm. She stared at him coldly until he lowered it. Vulpine looked at the eight men. "Your orders are changed. The man is not to be killed."

Their eyes narrowed at his words. He turned to Brianna knowing his words to the eight would not be heeded; their instructions came straight from Katarina, and nobody but she could countermand them. "Follow me."

Tears glazed Brianna's eyes, but she tilted her chin up and followed.

"I'll come for you," Mason called.

She nodded without turning.

I do not think so, Vulpine thought. If you do manage to live, you'll not move without pain for days, perhaps even weeks.

Mason watched the eyes of the eight men and knew without doubt they planned to kill him. He could have called the man leading Brianna away a liar to his face, but it would have solved nothing. This way, if things went bad, at least one of them still lived.

For how long? You know what Mirabella said. Rhonal wants Brianna dead. He hated the voice of

logic and reason inside his head and tried to put it away from him, but it went on.

You have not saved her in this lifetime either.

"Shut up," he snapped.

The eight men jumped at the sound of his voice.

"Will you kill me," he asked the nearest.

"Katarina has ordered your death."

"May I put the pup down first?"

The man nodded.

Mason put Gnaw down, then turned to the man and bowed. The man looked puzzled, then lowered his head and charged. The others held back, no doubt wanting to see the show.

Mason jumped to the side, stuck out his foot and the man sailed over it and landed face-first in the damp leaves and swampy ground. He rolled over onto his back. Black mud covered a good portion of his face. The other seven laughed and the part of his face not muddied filled with red.

"You'll not be laughing when Katarina skins you for a new vest," the man shouted.

Fear replaced amusement and, as one, they jumped forward.

Mason kicked, twisted, and chopped. Bones cracked and snapped. Screams filled the air. A foot found his ribs and pain lanced through him. A hand wrapped in his hair, jerked his head back. Hands closed around his throat. He reached out, found flesh, and dug his fingers into it. A hoarse scream sounded and still he dug. Warmth poured down his hands. The pressure at his throat loosened, and he dropped to the ground and rolled. He jackknifed up onto his feet and spun. Three still stood. The other five lay on the ground, either motionless or

writing.

The three eyed him. Then the one in the middle shrugged and turned away.

"What are you doing?" one of the others asked. "She'll kill us."

"And so will he, and he's here now," the one in the middle answered. "She isn't. I'll take my chances."

The man on Mason's right looked around clearly frightened. "If we run we can never go back..."

"Back to what? I have no children. My wife is dead. Out there I have a chance."

"But Rhonal?"

The man laughed. "The Dark God has more on his mind than one escaped slave."

"Two escaped slaves," the man to Mason's left said.

The two looked at the third. He looked from Mason to them. "I cannot kill him on my own."

"Then join with us, or return to Katarina."

"I cannot go back – she will know."

The two turned away, walked toward the trees. After a moment, the third followed.

Mason looked down at the five left. They were motionless now. He moved to each one and cautiously checked for a pulse. They were dead. It hit him then, and his knees shook. He'd never killed before. Always it had been sparring with his sensei. He stumbled three steps away, sunk to the ground, and vomited. Gnaw came to him, whined. Mason wiped his mouth and patted the top of the wolf pup's head. "We will get her back. I just have to figure out where to look."

Mirabella would know, but how was he to find

her? He took a deep breath and stood. One thing for sure, the answers weren't here, in the cottage, or the glade. He needed a weapon, a stout lance if nothing else. It wouldn't do him any good against the magic. For that, he'd need Mirabella, but if the bitch's other slaves were as human as this bunch, he could sure as hell do some major damage. And that shape-changing bastard would be the first. Damn, if his own powers weren't blocked from him, he'd show them a thing or two about magic. He had to find Mirabella. Mason slapped his leg. "Come on Gnaw." He was surprised to see the pup follow.

Chapter Seven

THE SHAPE-CHANGER, who told her his name was Vulpine, walked Brianna through a world of green: green trees, green grass, green brush, even the two birds she'd seen were green. So it startled her when he led her into an open meadow with a fairytale gone-amok castle in its center. The walls were a golden brick; a black wall of stone circled it. Turrets rose straight and tall, pennants flapped from their high peaks. The pennants were also black with some fantastical animal on them. She thought it might be a gryphon.

He led her toward a drawbridge. It was a narrow bridge, just big enough for the two of them to walk across side by side. Whatever was beneath it smoked and made her eyes water and burn.

They stopped before a portcullis of metal spikes, and Vulpine snorted in irritation. He glared up at the gatehouse. "Drago thinks to challenge me."

Brianna looked up toward the small balcony. A figure stood there, brown and glistening in the sun. As it turned to walk away, she clearly saw folded wings on its back.

The portcullis slowly lifted. Vulpine waited only until it cleared their heads before he waved her forward. Half through, she glanced up at the sharp points. How fast could it be lowered, she wondered?

The sweet smell of roses overpowered the stench of the moat. Curious, she looked ahead to a jungle of blooming roses – red, white, yellow, and every hue in between. Some clung to life-size

statues, obscuring their original shapes. Others spread into wide hedges.

"Oh, my God," Brianna said and almost gagged on the overpowering perfumes.

"Katarina likes roses," Vulpine said without expression.

Brianna held the back of her hand to her nose as she nodded.

"They are at lunch," Vulpine said. "We are to join them there." His voice was terse and angry as he stalked by her.

He set a quick pace and she did a fast jog to keep up with him. They passed through tall, ornate doors and down a hall with black walls and red tiles. Alabaster hands jutted from the walls, each held a lit candle. It was all too much. She was in sensory overload. It was like some Goth interior decorator had slipped over the edge into madness. She remembered a show from her youth, Captain Kangaroo. There'd been a cartoon on it, Fractured Fairytales. That's what this was, a Fractured Fairytale castle.

Vulpine stopped before two wide doors. He fairly bristled with animosity. He pushed the doors inward without knocking.

It was a dining hall. A large table stretched down its middle. A red table runner split it in half and silver candlesticks with black candles lined its center. Ornate carved chairs ran its length. A woman sat at one end of the table, and a man sat at the other. The woman's hair was red with streaks of gold. She wore a gown of shimmering ivory. Its neckline dipped low, showing an expanse of creamy skin. An emerald the size of a chicken's egg rested between her breasts. Her red-slicked lips smiled a

smile that didn't reach her cold, green eyes as Vulpine entered.

The man did not turn around.

Vulpine walked straight to her and bowed. "She is here as commanded, my queen."

The woman fixed Brianna with her frigid gaze. "Approach."

Brianna moved forward. The scent of roses came to her, and she swallowed. The woman extended a thin hand with dagger-like nails painted the same crimson as her mouth. Brianna took the offered hand, almost gasped as its heat burned her palm. The green gaze held hers for a moment, and then swept a glance over her. Brianna saw the judgment in the woman's eyes, no threat and unimportant. She felt her cheeks heat and she lifted her chin.

"I am Katarina, the future Queen of Alamonar." The woman's voice rang with arrogance.

"Brianna Cole."

"Yes, heir to the Ancient. I know who you are." Katarina waved a hand toward the end of the table. "My consort, Christian Samuels."

With Katarina's piercing gaze still upon her, she turned toward the man. He lifted a gold chalice toward her and then drank from it. So this was Mirabella's Christian. He wore a tunic of pale green. His long blond hair fell around his broad shoulders. She thought his eyes were brown, but then they changed to gold. He sat the chalice back down, and a servant scrambled to top it off with red wine.

"Charmed," he said, his words slurred.

Why, he's half-drunk, Brianna thought.

"We celebrate our betrothal this day,"

Katarina said.

Beside her, Brianna heard Vulpine groan.

"Oh? Congratulations," Brianna said.

Christian took another long drink of wine.

Katarina picked up her own chalice and sipped from it. "This will be the last I have for some time." A small, satisfied smile curved her lips. "I've heard spirits are not good for a breeding woman."

Christian laughed and Brianna looked sharply at him. What was going on here? He didn't look much like a prisoner to her. And was Katarina already pregnant by him? From where she stood, it looked like Mirabella was being played for a fool on all sides. Then Christian looked at her, and she saw the naked despair in his eyes.

"How is Mirabella?" Katarina said. "I would send an invitation to our early morning nuptials, but I do not think she would accept."

"I don't know what her schedule is for tomorrow," Brianna answered.

It was clear the woman didn't understand Brianna's meaning; anger glittered in her eyes. "Don't toy with me, girl. I had thought to only keep you from Mirabella until the Child of Prophecy is within me, but plans can be altered."

Brianna looked away from the piercing eyes. "I think you know where Mirabella is."

Katarina laughed. "The bitch shields herself well." She pushed away from the table and stood. "But it makes no difference. I have what she needs." She waved toward the table. "Are you hungry?"

Brianna shook her head. "No, thank you."

"Then I will have you shown to your room." A manservant hurried forward. "You will find it

comfortable, but a warning, do not try to leave. The results will be painful, to say the least."

She walked to Christian and held out her hand. "Come, love. I desire a walk in the garden."Christian did not rise, and Brianna saw red flood Katarina's face. "Must you always test me? I may not know where your fair Mirabella is at the moment, but she cannot hide from me forever."

With those words, Brianna understood the scene. It was an old story. She had the man leashed with her threats to his real love. She sighed. Agreements like that never worked.

In silence, she followed the servant. How was she going to get out of here? If she did manage to escape the castle, she had no idea where Mirabella's cottage was. It galled her to sit and wait, but there just didn't seem to be any other way to go.

They stopped before a door, and the man opened it and stepped back for her to enter. "Thank you," she said. The servant looked startled before he turned and hurried away.

Brianna crossed the room to a large open window. She was on the bottom floor of the castle and beyond the window was the rose garden. With a grimace, she closed the window. The room wasn't bad. Done up in shades of purple and gold, it was downright royal. The large canopied bed filled its center. A freestanding wardrobe and highboy stood to each side of the bed, and a tri-folding screen made up most of the left wall. The rugs were some kind of white, fluffy animal fur, and she took great pains to walk around them.

She moved to the wardrobe and opened it. Gowns hung on pegs inside. They were of all colors and made out of some silk-like fabric. She

wondered if Katarina kept dresses in all the bedrooms of the castle.

Brianna heard loud sharp words and walked back to the window. Beneath an arbor, Katarina and Christian stood. Braving the rose perfume, she opened the window a crack.

"Of course, a priest will marry us," Katarina said. "I've sent for one."

"A white priest will never come to you."

"I didn't say white, did I?"

Christian laughed. "So our marriage," he bitterly stressed the word, "will be unblessed?"

Katarina smiled. "Oh, we will be blessed, just not by Mirabella's Goddess Anete."

"She is my goddess, too."

Katarina reached up and brushed a strand of hair from his face." You must put her from your mind – the Goddess and Mirabella. Both Rhonal and I are jealous types."

Christian stepped back from her.

"Don't do that," she snapped. "You are to be my consort."

"You may have my body," he said, "but that is all you will ever have."

"Damn you. I can have her killed..."

"And if you do, I will kill you, my promise, not an idle threat.

"Kill me? To try will mean your own death." Katarina raised her voice.

"Yes, I know."

"What a fool you are, Christian Samuels. Do you think she cares for you? It is the Goddess Anete she obeys. If the Goddess had not told her to be with you, she would not be."

"You lie. We love each other, and have for

many lifetimes."

"She wants your child, the same as I do." Katarina spat the words at him.

"No, not the same. You wish to have Alamonar beneath your thumb. The Child of Prophecy will but a tool for you and Rhonal. Mirabella wants Alamonar to remain free."

Katarina spun away from him. "Make yourself ready for me."

"I thought we were to wait until after we were joined in union?" Christian cast a haunted look around the garden.

"I've changed my mind," Katarina snapped. "And what does it matter? You said it would mean nothing to you."

When he did not answer, she turned to face him again. "Do not worry; you will be able to perform. Your heart may not want me, but your body will."

Katarina sauntered by him with a pronounced sway of her hips. Halfway down the path, she turned and looked back. Christian stared at the ground, and Brianna laughed softly as the woman spun and stomped away.

Brianna watched until she was gone and then leaned out the window. "Christian."

Startled, he turned toward her window. With a glance behind him, he came to her. "You heard?"

"Yes."

His face flushed. "Things are not as they seem."

"I know how things are – you stay with her and Mirabella lives."

He smiled bitterly. "I am a fool to trust her." He gave her a sharp look. "As you are to believe that

you will live after the child is conceived. Rhonal is a vengeful god, and full of hatred to anything that remains of Sarunos."

"I know," Brianna said. "I heard her say you were to come to her tonight. Doesn't she know about the eclipse part of the program?"

"What?"

"The day becoming night," she reminded him.

"Katarina knows," he said with a defeated smile. "It is her way of punishment. I have displeased her."

"But what if she becomes pregnant before?"

"I don't know this word pregnant." He looked puzzled.

"With child," Brianna said.

"She will not, she is a sorceress."

"Oh. I get it." She looked across the rose garden. "Mason will come for us."

"He is the seeker?" Christian asked as his gaze searched her face.

Brianna nodded.

"He is dead."

Her heart thudded. "No, he isn't. I went with Vulpine so they would leave him alone."

Christian laughed. "Now who's the fool? Of course they killed him. Katarina told them to. It is beyond them to go against her orders."

Brianna swayed and tightened her hold on the windowsill. It wasn't true. Mason had to be alive; they'd just found each other again, and what about Gnaw? She held her breath and pictured him in her mind. In all the romance books, the heroine could feel if her love was dead. She felt nothing and released her breath with a disgusted snort. But stubbornness prevailed. He wasn't dead. Damn. Life

couldn't be that cruel. She looked at Christian, shook her head. "Mason can handle himself. We'll just have to wait and see who's right."

Christian looked at her in surprise, and then he smiled. "You are a strange woman, but for some reason, you give me hope. We will wait for our rescuers together, that is, until Katarina sends someone for me."

She stepped back from the window. "I'd ask you to come in, but with those magic things on the window..."

He reached a hand out and touched her cheek. "The wards only serve to keep one from going out, not someone from coming in."

*****

Vulpine watched Christian climb through the window and into Brianna's room. Katarina would not like that. Should he tell her? Jealousy alone would not keep Christian out of Katarina's arms, but it might buy him some time, and if they were to escape? For Mirabella to give birth to the Child of Prophecy would bring about Katarina's downfall. Would she turn to him then? The thought intrigued him as he turned and walked back into the garden.

Chapter Eight

Mason Stood At the edge of the glade and stared into the woods. In the cottage, he'd found a pair of cotton trousers and a tunic. Christian's, no doubt, and he thanked the Goddess. He'd had no wish to go searching for Mirabella skyclad.

At his feet, Gnaw whined. He reached down and touched the wolf pup's head. Anger and frustration made acid churn in his stomach. Which way should he go? How would he find Mirabella? He could stumble around for hours out there and never find her. What was Katarina doing to Brianna? By the Goddess, no; he wouldn't lose her to death again.

Gnaw moved away from him and into the first of the trees. She turned, looked back at Mason, and whined. The pup? The thought was stupid. Mason shrugged. He had no better idea.

They followed no trail, just wove in and out among the trees and brush. Three times he'd had to backtrack when a wall of brambles blocked them. Gnaw stopped, sniffed the air, and then yipped and bounded forward. Hope rose and then withered. Twice before the young pup had done so – and twice before it had been nothing. A sense of hopelessness weighted Mason's legs. How long had they walked? He looked toward the sun. It rode low on the horizon, its golden light already fading from the forest floor. Should he turn back? He'd been careful to mark his return trail to the cottage.

Ahead of him, Gnaw turned and yipped again. Okay, he'd hang in there a little longer, but if this

turned out to be another dead end, they were going back.

Gnaw danced along the bank of a swift-flowing stream. Mason groaned. "We've got to cross it?"

Gnaw lifted her head and howled. The wolf pup's surprised look at the sound made him smile.

He looked up and down the stream. He hadn't expected a bridge, but maybe some well-placed rocks. No such luck. He was going to get wet.

He frowned at Gnaw. "Mirabella damned-well-better-be on the other side of this."

Mason pulled first one shoe and sock from his foot, and then the other. Reaching down, he rolled his trousers high above his knees in a vain hope he could wade across the stream. Tying the shoelaces together, Mason draped them around his neck.

He grimaced as his bare toes touched the water. Somewhere, Alamonar had some snow-covered peaks because this stream felt like melted run-off. Gnaw yipped at him.

"What? I'm supposed to carry you?" He bent and picked up the pup. "You squirm one time and you're on your own."

Gritting his teeth, he waded in.

The frigid water rose. Twice he swore when stones rolled beneath his bare feet. When the water lapped his waist, he turned and glanced back. They were over half way. Gnaw whined her unease.

"Don't complain to me," he snapped."This was your idea." His toes found sand and the water level dropped. Soon it lapped his thighs.

He climbed up on to the dry bank and sat Gnaw down. She sniffed the air and then pranced to his right. "Alright. Alright."

A log lay higher up the bank and he walked to it and put on his shoes and socks. He stood, rolled down his trouser legs, grimaced as they clung to his wet skin.

"Lead on, McDuff," he said with a wave of his hand, and Gnaw darted forward.

They walked another quarter of a mile before they found her. Mirabella sat at the base of a large oak tree. Her head did not turn as they neared. They stopped in front of her and still she did not say a word. Gnaw touched her hand with her nose and Mirabella blinked. Her hand rose to scratch behind Gnaw's left ear, and it was then she looked up. Quick surprise and then anger crossed her face.

"What are you doing here? You should have never left the glade." He saw it in her eyes, the instant she realized Brianna wasn't with them. "By the Goddess, no. Katarina has her, but how?"

"She tossed slave after slave at the wards until they dissolved. I saw their bodies, and then a shape-changer and eight more of them found us."

"How long has she had Brianna?" Mirabella leaned back to look up at him.

"I'm not sure. At least three hours. I've been looking for you since then. I wouldn't have found you except for Gnaw."

Mirabella nodded. "We connected when I searched for Katarina's taint within her." She stroked the wolf pup. "It is good she found Brianna." For a moment, her eyes unfocused. "I do wonder why the Goddess did not warn me...but it is not for me to question."

She held out her hand, and Mason drew her to her feet. "But they are together now, Christian and Brianna. Maybe it is as the Goddess willed."

"So where is Katarina's cottage, and how do we get them back?"

Mirabella sighed. "I'm afraid it isn't a cottage, but a castle with all of its armaments."

"How many slaves?" he asked.

"An army," she replied, "and all will die for her. Her magic is strong within its walls."

Mason frowned. "And there's Rhonal, too."

Mirabella shrugged. "Rhonal has his own desires. He would sacrifice Katarina to us in a instant if it furthered them." Her forehead creased. "We cannot overpower them, and her magic will counteract mine. Stealth is the only way. But there is one within the walls who might help."

"Who?"

"Vulpine, the shape-changer. He desires Katarina."

"And Christian stands in his way."

She nodded. "The Goddess sees him as a weakness in the castle. We must use him, but how? What do I do to push him to aid us?" Gnaw nudged her hand and Mirabella smiled. "Yes, little one. I see the Goddess' plan." She faced Mason. "We will send Gnaw to Brianna."

He frowned. "What can she do?"

"I will put the magic inside her. It will be brought forth when Vulpine touches Gnaw."

"Won't Katarina feel your magic?" He didn't like the sound of her plan, but what other choice did they have?

A smile lit her face. "Maybe, but she will not suspect a pup. She will look for its cause beyond the castle walls."

"Your magic inside Gnaw, once it's unleashed, will weaken all inside so we can get to Brianna and

Christian?"

Mirabella shook her head. "Impossible. What it will do is push Vulpine's jealousy over the edge. He is the key."

"So we must sit on our hands and wait and hope?" He snapped out the words.

She touched his arm. "I see it chafes you, but you will see action. More than you care to. Even when Christian and Brianna are freed, Rhonal and Katarina will not take it lightly."

She looked up at the setting sun. "And we've another day before I can brew the potion to make Sarunos a part of me." She turned toward the trees. "Come, we must go back to my cottage. What I need for my magic is there."

Mason looked down at the wolf pup. "It won't hurt Gnaw, will it?"

"The magic will not – beyond that I have no control."

He frowned and bent to pick up Gnaw. She whined and licked his cheek. "Brianna won't like it if something happens to her."

"The Goddess watches over her own."

"You don't know another way back to the cottage, do you?" he asked with a grimace, "one that doesn't involve wading across a very cold stream?"

"Wading? No, we must cross the stream. But we will not wade. Levitation, my boy. Levitation."

Chapter Nine

BRIANNA AND CHRISTIAN stood side-by-side in the window and watched the darkness spread and settle across the rose garden.

She glanced up at him. "She'll send for you soon, won't she?"

He sighed. "I fear so."

"I wish..."

"I know, but it cannot be helped." He touched her arm. "She can use my body, but she can never have my heart."

Brianna blinked back tears. He placed an arm around her shoulders and pulled her against his side. "Don't weep for me."

The door slammed against the wall and they both jumped apart.

"Touching little scene, isn't it?" Katarina coldly snapped. "What would Mirabella think of this?" She moved to stand in front of Brianna and then lifted her hand and slapped her across the face. "Whore."

With a cry, Brianna stumbled back.

Katarina whirled to face Christian. "Why will you lift everybody's skirt but mine?"

Christian stepped between Brianna and Katarina. "Leave her alone. We did nothing."

Two men came through the door. Katarina pointed at Brianna. "Strip her and take her below." She looked at Brianna with contempt. "I had thought to treat you as a guest, and this is how you thank me."

The taller of the two men stepped forward.

Brianna watched his avid gaze move across her body. "What then, mistress?"

Katarina smiled. "Use her as you wish."

"Rhonal will not want her dead," Vulpine said, stepping into the room.

"They will not kill her." She glared at the man. "Will you?"

"She'll live." He took a step toward Brianna.

Christian whirled, grabbed an ornate vase and slammed it against the windowsill. Its top half shattered and he thrust its jagged edge toward the man. "You will not do this, Katarina."

"Do not tell me what I can do," Katarina ground out between clenched teeth. "Take him."

The man lunged forward and Christian lashed out. The attacker bellowed and stumbled back, blood spurted from a wide gash in his upper arm.

"You dare damage what is mine?" She pointed a finger at Christian, and he screamed and dropped to his knees.

"No," Brianna screamed.

He looked up at her with dazed eyes.

"How touching," Katarina said.

Large, calloused hands grabbed Brianna by her shoulders. Fingers dug deep into her flesh.

"Get up," Katarina yelled and shoved Christian with the toe of her slipper. He tried, made it up to his knees and then collapsed again onto his stomach.

She whirled to rage at Brianna. "Now see what you have done. He will be of no use to me this night."

She glared back at Christian. "You desired her. Then look at what you will never have." She pointed at Brianna. "Strip her now."

Brianna twisted away from the man who held her and stumbled back.

Katarina laughed. "You cannot run."

Brianna's chin went up. "You want me naked? Then I'll do it myself."

She reached for the hem of her blouse and drew it up and over her head. She bunched it into a ball and threw it at Katarina's feet. The air was cool upon her bare breasts, and her nipples tightened. The men's gazes moved over her. Feeling sick inside, she pushed the long skirt down. It pooled at her feet, and with a sharp kick, she sent it flying across the room. She refused to cringe, and instead thrust her shoulders back and looked straight into Katarina's eyes.

The nearest man reached out. "I will have her first."

The second elbowed him aside and the two turned to glare at each other, snarls upon their lips.

"Pathetic fools," Katarina snarled. "Draw lots for her."

"I think not," Vulpine said and moved by them. "She will be mine."

He stopped in front of Brianna and ran his fingers along her arm. "She interests me."

Brianna closed her eyes, but didn't jerk away. He would be better than the two other brutes.

"You want her?"

Brianna snapped her eyes open at Katarina's sharp question.

Vulpine smiled. "Look at her." He walked around Brianna. "Her body will provide me hours of amusement."

Inside, she quailed at his choice of words, but she refused to let them see her fear.

"I'd think you'd have better taste."

Brianna felt a hand thrust into the middle of her back. It pushed and she stumbled forward and then fell onto her knees.

"Then take her out of my sight."

She heard the two other men grumble.

"You will have her," Katarina snapped. "Send for them when you are finished with the whore. She will be kept busy this night spreading her legs."

"She will be well used," Vulpine said. "Perhaps they may have her tomorrow. It depends on when I grow tired of her."

Hands closed around her arms, and helped her to her feet. She stood, faced Vulpine. Her eyes searched his, and he gazed back coldly.

"Come," he said, and then turned his back and walked away. She heard Katarina laugh as she trailed after him. As she passed the first man, he reached out and pinched her right nipple. With a gasp, she raked her fingernails down his cheek. He screamed and lifted his hand to strike her.

In an instant, Vulpine was between them. "If she is to be bruised, it will be my pleasure to do so."

The man brought his hand to his bleeding cheek instead. "Yes, Vulpine." His words were meek, but the gaze he fastened on her promised reprisal.

"Follow me," Vulpine said.

His room looked much the same as the one Katarina had given her: a bed, a wardrobe, a small round table, and a screen that shielded the chamber pot. He walked to the wardrobe, opened it, and turned to her with a red gown hanging over his arm. He tossed it to her. Brianna caught it. "Katarina keeps gowns in every chamber." he said.

She slipped it over her head. "Why?" The dress brushed the floor and her breasts strained against the too-small top. The low-cut bodice bared her flesh almost to the nipples.

"Why does she keep gowns in each?" He smiled as he finished the words.

"No. Why did you take me away from them?"

He stared at her silence for a long moment. "I don't know. It was an impulse." He crossed the room and stared out the window. "You look quite fetching in that gown. How do you know I will not rape you?"

"Will you?" Pain shot through her cheek and she lifted her hand to trace a tender, puffy area.

"I want Katarina, no other."

Brianna ran her fingers through her disheveled hair. "She didn't seem to care when you took me."

He turned to face her. "It looked to be so."

She noticed a pitcher on the small table. "May I have something to drink?"

He waved a hand toward it. "Help yourself, but then it would probably be best if you did a little screaming, they will be listening for it."

Brianna nodded as she walked to the table. A mug stood behind the pitcher. She poured water to its brim and then drank until it was almost empty. "Thank you," she said, and then screamed piercingly. She waited a moment and then did it again, adding a loud. "No, please, no."

"Very nice." He moved to a curtained alcove and jerked it open. Three men stood there, each holding a lute. "Play." A lilting tune began. "She knows I like music when I make love." He motioned her close and grinned when she hesitated.

Squaring her shoulders, she came to stand in

front of him.

"Now straining ears will not hear our words. Please scream again."

She obliged him.

"I wish to thank you."

Her surprise made her cut off the cry in mid chord. "What?"

Vulpine smoothed his tunic. "I had grown impatient and angry with jealousy but, thanks to you, I have seen that Christian will never love Katarina as she desires. She may force him to lie with her, but she will never have his heart."

"He loves Mirabella."

"I had thought to risk much and help the two of you escape."

Her heart thudded as he said it, but he dashed her hopes with his next words. "But I see now I need not. Patience will bring Katarina to me. She will tire of wooing Christian."

Brianna closed her eyes for a moment, then opened them and stared into his. "What about me?"

"I can offer you a reprieve for this night, but..." He looked toward the closed door.

"Then she will give me to those men."

Vulpine nodded. "Not just them, but many others."

She pressed her hands to her stomach.

"Katarina did not lie when she said she would not kill you – Rhonal wishes to do so himself." He laughed. "Mirabella thinks the other gods will stay his hand, but it will not be so. Rhonal desires the last of Sarunos' blood to be no more. For the sake of peace, they have agreed to give him what he craves, but he must kill you before the child is conceived. Which would have been this night, but...."

His words sent a shiver along her spine. How would a god choose to kill someone? Would her sudden death be enough, or would Rhonal wish it prolonged and painful?

Vulpine went on. "Christian she will keep as a pet. She will enjoy flaunting him before Mirabella."

Brianna swallowed. "What about the child?"

He shrugged. "Once Alamonar is hers, I do not know what will become of the Child of Prophecy, although I cannot see Katarina as a mother. Can you?" He smiled.

She shook her head.

He waved toward the bed. "Rest awhile. I will return." He walked to the door. "And do not try to leave this room. It would be painful."

She watched in silence as he closed the door behind him. A reprieve, but for how long? She walked to the window and looked out. Again, it was the rose garden. Was there any other view in this place?

A shudder started at her toes and worked up her body. She wrapped her arms around her and held on as she trembled. Christian's words came back to her and she shook her head in denial. No, Mason wasn't dead. He couldn't be. He would come for her. It would be different this time – this time he would be able to save her from death. Tears blurred her view and she didn't bother to wipe them away. "Please, Mason, please."

*****

Vulpine picked a rose, held it to his nose, and breathed in the ripe sweetness. His words to Brianna had been calm, his proclaimed path the right one, but he had lied. The thought of Christian with Katarina, their bodies joined, his seed giving

her a child, made him burn with hatred. He shredded the rose, dropped the petals at his feet and ground his heels into them.

Vulpine stared at his trembling hands, then closed his eyes and drew in deep breaths. No. He was right. Katarina would tire of her new plaything. He had only to wait.

A rose bush to the side of him rustled. His eyes snapped open and he turned to stare. A pup came from beneath it. "Well, look at you." He picked it up. "Whose child do you belong to?"

The pup looked into his eyes, and for a moment his head filled with a warm buzzing. Vulpine swayed and the pup jumped from his arms and fled down a path. He frowned as he rubbed at his forehead.

Impatience surged. Brianna and Christian had to go. Why should he have to wait? He'd waited long enough already. With their freedom, the Child of Prophecy would be born to Mirabella. True, it would bring Katarina down, but then he would be there for her to turn to. His earlier plan was a coward's way. To achieve his end, there was but one course, he would help them escape.

Chapter Ten

BEYOND THE CASTLE'S wards of magic, Mason and Mirabella waited, she upon a fallen log, he pacing back and forth, the grass beneath his shoes flat and muddy.

"Mason, be still. You will wear yourself thin before action is needed." She kept her words soft, but stern.

He glanced at the dark sky. The first stars studded its blackness. His reply was just as low and cautious, but thick with frustration. "How much longer?"

She shrugged. "Until Gnaw returns."

A branch caught his sleeve and he jerked away. "How do we know the magic will work?"

"You saw the pup make it beyond the wards. She has but to find Vulpine."

"And if she doesn't?"

Mirabella shook her head. "Trust the Goddess."

He frowned. "The Goddess has separated us before, many times."

She touched his arm. "I have seen it. You and your love will be together..."

"But for how long?" He pulled away. "We've always been happy for awhile."

"A short time of happiness is better than a lifetime of bitterness."

He grimaced. "Mirabella, please. Don't feed me such fodder. I want a lifetime with Brianna. I will not accept any other way."

"The Goddess Anete..." she began again.

Mason cut her off. "The Goddess is sometimes wrong."

"Mason, we must wait. Vulpine will bring them to us, and then our struggle truly begins."

*****

Brianna jumped as the door slammed open. Vulpine walked into the room. Without a glance at her, he said. "I have decided you must leave."

"What?"

"It suits me to have you and Christian gone."

Her heart beat fast in hope, but fear urged caution. Why his change of mind?

He looked at her. "Why do you just stand there? You want to leave, don't you?"

She nodded.

"Then be ready. I am going for Christian."

She watched him turn and walk from the room. Just like that? He expected no one to stop him? She wrapped her arms around her body and paced. Minutes passed. Brianna moved closer to the door. How near could she get without disturbing the wards? She stopped while still a good distance away and strained to listen. A man walked by, looked into the room and met her gaze. His face was full of resigned despair and it chilled her. Was that what Katarina's reign as queen would bring to all?

She heard raised voices. Her stomach churned, and then Vulpine came back through the door gripping the arm of a dazed Christian.

"Hurry," Vulpine snapped. "They have not tried to stop me, but will soon go to Katarina to ask about my escorting her fair guest around the rose garden."

She noticed a puffy, red splotch upon Christian's jaw line.

"He doubted my offer," Vulpine said, and then smiled. "I had to help him make up his mind." He turned and jerked Christian back toward the door. "Walk at my other side. And try to look adoring. We have just spent some wonderful time upon my bed."

Christian looked at her and she felt her face heat. Let him think what he wanted. There wasn't time for explanations.

"If we are stopped, remain quiet," Vulpine said. "I am treating you to a walk in the garden and a visit with your other lover. That is all any need to know."

Her other lover? My, my, I've been a busy girl.

She followed him out the door and took her place at his side, proud her legs didn't shake too much. They passed the man who'd looked into her room earlier. She hoped the look she gave Vulpine was adoring and didn't look like she had a bad case of indigestion.

They made it into the moonlight-drenched garden before a shout came from behind them. They turned. The man she'd scratched earlier ran toward them.

"What's going on here?" he demanded.

From somewhere in Vulpine's clothing, a knife appeared. It flew straight and true, and the man crumbled with it embedded in his throat.

"I never cared for him," Vulpine said. "Follow close."

Dry-mouthed, Brianna nodded as Vulpine jerked her around and guided them toward a smaller, narrow path. The moon's glow lit their way. She glanced at Christian. His eyes had cleared and he seemed at last to accept Vulpine's help to freedom.

They came to a small gate in the wall. Vulpine touched it, waited a moment, and then pushed it open. "Go." He looked hard at Christian. "If we meet again, I will kill you. Katarina is mine."

Christian walked through the gate, looked around, and motioned for her. Stunned, she stared for a moment at Vulpine, opened her mouth to say thank you but, with a scowl, he turned on his heels and hurried away.

They stood at the edge of the forest. Silver light frosted the tall trees and a breeze blew, softly smelling of pine and flowers. Thank God, it isn't roses. Christian held a finger to his lips and pointed to the right. He moved out ahead of her. Silently, she followed.

The hem of her gown brushed the tall grass as she walked, and in moments, its chill dampness clung to her ankles and calves. She heard a bird's trill, and Christian stopped in front of her. By the moon's light, she watched him close his eyes, his forehead creased as he lifted his right hand, palm up.

"What are you doing," Brianna asked as a shiver moved up into her stomach.

He held a finger to his lips in answer and pointed toward a dark bush. Its leaves rustled and a nose poked through. Brianna drew back and then smiled as the rest of Gnaw's head emerged. The wolf pup sniffed the air and then bounded from the brush and ran to her. Brianna knelt and scratched behind Gnaw's ears as the wolf pup wiggled in delight.

"Yeah, I'm glad to see you, too. Did you bring Mason with you?"

"Mirabella comes," Christian said close to her

ear. She saw his look focus on a large tree trunk as Mirabella came from behind it.

Brianna blinked. A glow surrounded the other woman. It pulsed as she came toward them. Without words, Christian moved to meet her. They stared into each other's eyes for a long moment, then he opened his arms and she walked into them. She rested her cheek on his chest and he kissed the top of her head.

Tears filled Brianna's eyes and a lump formed in her throat.

"Brianna."

The spoken word drew her gaze back to the tree. Mason stood there. She moved toward him, her footsteps as first slow, and then, with a low sob, she ran the last few feet. His arms closed around her, pulled her close against his chest, and she felt him tremble. Her arms circled his waist and she pressed closer yet. If she could have, she would have crawled inside him. His heartbeat thudded against her cheek.

"Again, I almost lost you." She heard him whisper into her hair.

She tilted her head back and looked into his face. "But you didn't. We're together."

He ran his hands down the length of her arms. "Did she hurt you?" His lips tensed as he touched her bruised jaw.

"It could've been worse." She turned her head and looked across to Christian and Mirabella. "What now?"

"We've talked," Mason said. "This night belongs to us. Tomorrow…" His words trailed off and he shrugged. "Tomorrow we do what is required."

Their arms looped around each other's waists,

Mirabella and Christian turned toward the trees. "Where are they going?" Brianna said.

"To be alone," Mason said. "The cottage is ours until sunrise."

Gnaw yipped. "Well, ours and Gnaw's."

"But they can't make love, not until tomorrow during the eclipse."

Mason smiled. "True, they can't have sex until then, but there is much more to lovemaking than the final act of conceiving."

He stepped back from her and reached to take her hand. A curious sense of shyness moved through her as she laced her fingers with his and let him draw her forward.

At the cottage door, Mason hesitated. He turned to face her and clasped both her hands. Gnaw, who had trotted before them, now yipped and continued toward the backyard. She watched in bemusement as the wolf pup disappeared around the corner and then recognized the Goddess' hand in providing the two of them with some private time. "Brianna," Mason said. "I have loved you in many lifetimes, and will continue to do so throughout eternity. "

His words made her breath catch in her throat. Unable to speak, she nodded and gave his hands a squeeze.

"Our love before has always been blessed by both the church and the Goddess." He lifted her hands and kissed each one. "In my heart, we are already joined, but before we go inside, I will give to you my vows so that the gods themselves will know of my commitment to you."

She felt a chill move along the back of her neck. Were Mason's words a challenge to Rhonal?

Aftermath

Still holding her hands, he knelt before her and lifted their linked fingers to rest against his heart. His gaze held hers as he spoke. "You hold it within your hands."

If someone else had said those words to her, she would have laughed in his face, but here and now, they seemed right. She swallowed and licked her lips. "And you've got mine."

Mason smiled. "You are my other half. I am not complete without you."

She felt her knees begin to shake.

"Here, before all," Mason said. "I declare my love and take you for my wife." He reached inside a pocket and held his hand out toward her. In his palm lay the warded charm of bone.

"Not much of a wedding gift, but priceless under the circumstances." He slipped the braided cord over her head.

Brianna closed her eyes for a moment and inhaled deeply. When she opened them, a serene calm flowed through her. Her knees strengthened, and the words came clear and strong. "Mason Warren, I love you. I feel it in my soul that we are meant to be together. And here, before all, I declare my love and take you as my husband."

He released her hands, put his arms around her waist, and pulled her close. They stood in silence, her ear pressed against his heart. Then Mason stepped back, clasped her hand and drew her into the cottage.

*****

Warm lips nuzzled Brianna's shoulder and, with eyes still closed, she laughed. She lifted her hands and her eyes flew open as her fingers burrowed into soft fur. Golden eyes stared back at her, and then Gnaw yipped and swiped her tongue

the length of Brianna's cheek.

"Hey," Brianna said as she wiped her face. "I love you, too." She looked around the cottage. "Where's Mason?"

She stretched and then groaned. Their lovemaking last night had been vigorous. Her face heated as some of the Mason's more inventive techniques played themselves over in her mind, and she hadn't been too bad herself.

He walked in the cottage door and, seeing her awake, grinned. "Good morning."

Her gaze moved over him. He wore nothing but a pair of trousers. They were damp and clung to his thighs. His bare chest glistened and his long hair grazed his shoulders. She remembered its silkiness beneath her fingers and how it fell forward to frame his face as he lay atop her.

She felt a flame ignite in her stomach. She couldn't believe how she wanted him right now. She'd never considered herself particularly sexual. She'd had lovers before, but could never figure out what the big deal was. She sure had never felt the over-the-top, star-seeing climax the romance books talked about – that is, until last night. Oh, yeah, she was sexual. She just needed the right lover to show her.

"Had a bath in the lake," he said.

"I could use one of those."

"Maybe I could join you?"

Brianna licked her lips. "You just had a dip."

He reached out his hand toward her. "One can never be too clean."

She grasped it and let him pull her to her feet. The chill air brought her nipples to attention.

"Cold, my love?"

Before she could answer, he lowered his head and took one of her nipples into his mouth. She gasped as his warm tongue circled it. Pleasure arced through her, and her knees threatened to buckle. She pressed closer against his solid length and felt him swell hotly against her rib cage. His mouth switched to her other breast as his hands moved to clasp her hips and rotate her against him. Behind her, she heard Gnaw whine, and then the wolf pup bounded by and toward the cottage door.

"Mason? Brianna?" She heard Mirabella's voice call. With a squeak, Brianna pulled back from Mason, whirled and dove back beneath the coverings.

"May we come in," Mirabella asked.

"Of course," Mason said.

Mirabella entered, Christian following behind. Gnaw yipped and wiggled as if she'd just been reunited with lost friends until Brianna patted the quilt and called to her.

She watched Mirabella look from Mason's face to hers. A knowing look entered the sorceress' eyes and she smiled. "I trust you are well rested?"

Brianna hurried to answer before Mason did. "Yes, very much, and you?"

"As rested as you are, I am sure."

The two women exchanged self-satisfied smiles.

Brianna heard a stifled snort of laughter and looked sharply at Mason, who quickly said. "What is the first thing to do today?"

Mirabella sighed. "Katarina will seek us."

"And Rhonal?" Mason said.

"No doubt the dark god will guide her. Neither will wish the spell to be completed," Christian said.

Mason looked at Mirabella. "You have a plan?"

She touched his shoulder. "You will be our weapon."

Mason looked perplexed. "What do you mean?"

"It is your magik that will defeat Katarina."

Mason frowned. "My magik is blocked from me in Alamonar."

"It is, but you too will drink of the Goddess Anete's potion, and your magik will open to you and your commands. This Katarina does not know." She turned to take Christian's hand. "Even I did not know of this until last night. We will go to a place chosen by the Goddess. Its location has been blurred from Rhonal's search until the Goddess wishes for us to be seen. There we will await Katarina."

Chapter Eleven

KATARINA LIFTED HER arms and her hair rose around her, writhed as if alive. Lightning sparks flashed from strand to strand within it. "Gone? What do you mean gone?" she said to the man who groveled at her feet.

"When we went to get him, the room was empty." The words were spoken into the floor.

Vulpine. The surety of how Christina escaped flowed through her. "And the bitch?"

"Vulpine's bed is empty."

"And where is my loyal shape-shifter this morn?" she ground through gritted teeth.

"He has not been seen."

"Rise," she said. The man's first bungled attempts to stand pleased her. She looked into his ashen face. "You have displeased me." She smelled the acrid bite of urine as his bladder failed.

"Yes, Mistress." He pulled a knife from the sheath at his side and held it out to her.

"You do it."

His lips trembled. "How do you wish it? Stomach or throat?"

She smiled. " I leave the choice to you. Will it be slow or fast?"

He lifted the knife to his throat. Where the blade touched a thin red line formed. Blood trickled down his neck.

"Stop," she said with a frown. "You will make a mess." Her lips thinned at the hope that flickered in his eyes." I'll give you one chance to redeem yourself. Bring Vulpine to me."

At her words, the ember of hope died, and with a flash, he sliced across his throat. Blood gushed, drenched her with warmth. Cursing, Katarina stepped back as he fell. What a waste. She would make Christian take his place for a while before she forgave and allowed him back into her bed. She called out and the door opened. Three guards came into the room.

"Remove that," she ordered.

"Yes, Mistress." They scrambled to remove the body of the man who until this morn had been their superior.

She pointed at one in random. "You will take his place. All will answer to you, and you will answer to me." The blood drained from his face as he nodded. "My first command for you is to find Vulpine. I wish to speak with him."

The man stiffened and then reached for the knife at his side.

"No," she snapped. "It is a request and not an order. He may come to me at his earliest convenience."

The man removed his hand from the knife and bowed. "Yes, Mistress."

Fool, she thought, as he backed toward the door. I should have let him cut his own throat, but I will need every man when I am in control of Alamonar.

The blood still pooled on the stone floor. With distaste, she stepped over it. "Clean this up," she barked at the two men who remained as she exited the room.

Aftermath

*****

Katarina pulled another rose from the bush, shredded it with her nails, then ground the yellow petals into the dirt with the toe of her boot. Wilted splotches of yellow surrounded her. The day was half over and she had accomplished nothing. Vulpine had not come, and all her appeals to Rhonal had been ignored. The dark god's silence chilled her. For hours, she'd gone over her actions of the past days in her mind, and in none could she find things that would have angered him. Then why the silence between them?

"Katarina?"

She whirled at the word. Vulpine stood behind her. How had he gotten so close without her awareness? Her irritation rose. "Vulpine."

"You wished to see me?"

"Our guests are gone – both of them."

He cocked an eyebrow and waited.

"The news does not surprise you?"

She held a rose out toward him. He took it and inhaled its fragrance. "I'd heard they were gone. Do you think they went together?"

Her eyes narrowed as she said. "It would seem so."

The question was there between them – had he helped them in their escape? Each knew the answer.

"The guard who let it happen has been dealt with," she said.

"The eclipse is today," Vulpine said.

She dropped the rose she held. "Yes."

"And Rhonal has told you his wishes?"

She looked away from him. "I know what must be done."

"How may I serve you?"

"I am waiting to find out the whereabouts of the bitch Mirabella. She has shielded herself from me. Rhonal will tell me soon. The..."

He interrupted her. "I know where they are. I have just returned."

Her head jerked toward him. "Oh, my loyal Vulpine. What would I do without you? Are they far from us?"

He glanced up into the sky. "Far enough that the eclipse could be upon us before we are upon them."

"We've hours before..."

"Look." He pointed upward.

She frowned. "I see nothing."

"It has begun. I already feel the call of the night." He stretched his neck from side to side as it to relieve stiffness.

"Then why do we stand here? Take me to them."

"We will cover more area if you shape-shift." His words held a challenge.

Katarina could not resist her urge to play coy. "What do you wish me to become? A vixen?"

Vulpine shrugged. "The choice is yours."

His indifference made her flush and she reached out and placed her hand against his heart. He tensed at her touch and she felt his heartbeat accelerate. Yes, he still desired her. The thought appeased her, but the anger still simmered. How dare he make her doubt herself? Along with Rhonal's continued silence, it became almost more than she could take.

Vulpine would pay. She would make him watch as Christian made love to her, he and

Mirabella, too. The thoughts made her smile. She watched his eyes narrow as she smiled, and that pleased her even more, but her smile faded as he turned from her and began his shape-shift. Fog rose from the ground, shrouded him, red lightning flickered inside the gray-white cloud. Then it melted into the ground as fast as it had formed.

The fox stood before her. His golden eyes stared up at her, the challenge still there. With a grimace, she began her own change, felt the instant itch as hair sprouted and the pain as her bones shortened and changed skeletal shape.

Her senses came alive, the air sweeter, bringing with it the scents of voles and rabbits. With a laugh, she willed her vixen form into heat, swung her tail back and forth.

Vulpine's mind-voice came to her, the tone harsh. "Do you really want to do that? I am not the only fox in these woods. Do you wish to waste time with mating battles?"

She bared her teeth at him. He was right. This was not the time, but she added it to the growing list of things he would later be punished for. She lifted a paw and held it out toward him. Even in her fox form, a greenish-black shroud hovered around each claw's pointed end.

"An addition to my wardrobe," she said. "One scratch will be the end of any who stand in my way. And it will not be a pretty death."

Vulpine said nothing, instead turned and bounded into the trees. She growled, and with an irate flick of her tail, followed.

Chapter Twelve

BRIANNA LOOKED AROUND. They'd walked for hours, crossed streams and wound among trees. Mirabella had apologized at the first stream, saying she could not levitate them across. Her magik had to be saved for the potion. Now they stood before yet another grove of oaks. The sun rose high in the clear, opaque blue of the sky. She saw no changes; the sun still beat hotly upon the top of her head, but she'd seen the worried glances Mirabella had cast upward as the time passed. Had the eclipse begun?

Brianna shaded her eyes with her hand and looked harder at the trees. Where their shadows shorter?

"Remove your clothing," Mirabella said.

Brianna jerked her gaze to her. "What?"

"We go to the Goddess Anete as we came into the world," she said. Christian was busy with the laces that held Mirabella's gown together in the back. He stepped away as Mirabella reached for her skirt hem and began to shed his own clothing.

Brianna glanced at Mason. He'd already removed his tunic and was undoing the drawstring at his wait. The gown she wore laced in the front and, with an inward shrug, she untied the first bow. In moments, the four stood naked. With a natural, easy grace, Mirabella moved to the nearest tree. She closed her eyes. Sweet sounds came from her mouth; they couldn't be called words, more like bird trills. When she finished, she lifted her hand, kissed her fingers and then touched the trunk of the tree.

"The Goddess will open to us now," she said and stepped back. "We enter into her womb of creation."

Questions crowded Brianna's mind. She opened her mouth to ask them, but Mirabella's second worried glance into the sky made her stop. If there were time afterward, she would get her answers, and if there was not, then the answers were not important.

Mirabella waved them forward.

Brianna wasn't sure what she expected, another kind of gate into a fantastical setting, and her body did tingle as she passed the oak tree, but the glade looked no different than the others they moved through. The tall grass swayed in the gentle breeze, flowers dotted its green with blue and yellow, and a fallen tree lay to the right. Then she recognized the scene. It was the glade from the painting that hung in Mason's gallery. She moved to the tree and looked for the brown and black knothole. Tracing it with her fingers, she searched the area behind the tree. The small mound of dirt was there and, as she stared, a tiny brown head poked up. The color of the ground squirrel's eyes surprised her, they were bright green. Had she noticed before?

Mirabella stopped beside her. "Goddess, we are here."

Startled, Brianna looked at her. Mirabella spoke to the ground squirrel. She heard no reply, but Mirabella nodded and turned to Brianna. "It is time to begin. The eclipse will be upon us in less than two hours' time."

Mirabella suddenly moaned and swayed.

Christian leapt to catch her in his arms.

"What is it?" Brianna said.

"Rhonal has broken through the Goddess' shielding ward. Katarina will be coming."

With the words, goose bumps erupted on Brianna's arms.

The ground squirrel came completely from its burrow. It circled the tree and stopped before Mason. With gentle care, Mason picked it up and placed it on the fallen tree between Mirabella and Brianna.

Brianna's stomach quivered. "What now?"

"We take your blood," Mirabella said.

How? They were all naked, and she didn't see a knife anywhere. Was the ground squirrel goddess going to bite her?

"Will it hurt?" She felt hands upon her shoulders and looked up into Mason's eyes.

Mirabella smiled. "There will be no pain. Do you wish a mark to be left?"

"What?"

"The Goddess can leave a remembrance to always remind you of your part in the saving of Alamonar, or not."

Brianna didn't think she needed something to remember all this, but why not? She nodded as she held up her hand. The little groundhog began to chant, its voice clear and sweet. Mirabella took Brianna's hand and turned it over so her wrist lay skyward. Brianna felt her heart beat fast. Around her, the light began to dim, but it wasn't the red and orange of a sunset, but a dull gray instead. She started to look up.

"No," Mason said, "The eclipse has started. You will hurt your eyes. See the birds."

She looked toward the nearest tree. Birds had lighted and were tucking their heads beneath their wings.

"They think night is coming," Mason said.

Brianna's warming skin drew her gaze back to her wrist. She blinked and then blinked again. The skin just above her wrist was separating. It wasn't like a cut; it was like her wrist opened. The line was small, barely an inch in length. She watched a drop of blood rise from the opening and float in the darkening around them; a second and then a third joined it.

Mirabella held out a small round bowl. It looked as if it was made of living leaves. A yellow liquid bubbled inside. The blood floated down into the bowl and then sank into the yellow.

"Mason?" Brianna said with a tremble in her voice.

She felt his hands squeeze her shoulders. "You will be fine."

Her wrist flared hotly and she gasped. As she stared, her skin flowed back together. A red splotch formed and, as it faded, she saw the mark; it was etched in gold and was the shape of a tiny teardrop. "Oh."

"Mason, drink," Mirabella said and held the bowl out to him. Only a small portion of the potion remained.

He took the bowl from her and lifted it to his lips.

Brianna looked from Mason to Mirabella. They didn't look any different.

Mirabella reached to take Christian's hand. An almost complete blackness coated the glade now. The two of them walked toward a large willow tree

she hadn't noticed before now.

She felt Mason draw her back against him. She turned in his arms. His mouth found hers. The kiss was soft. She parted her lips and his tongue slipped inside. His hands moved down her back, settled on each hip and pulled her closer against him. He lifted his head. She could just see his face in the darkness.

He smiled. "My magik is awake." Still holding each other, they sank into the grass. How could they be doing this now when Katarina and Vulpine stalked them? But they were.

Their lovemaking was slow and sweet.

As she sighed with pleasure, she heard a soft whine and felt Gnaw snuggle against her legs. Mason's chest rose as his breath lifted the hair at her temple.

"It is done. The Child of Prophecy is conceived."

Chapter Thirteen

"*IT IS OVER,*" Rhonal's voice said in Katarina's mind. "*The bloodline of Sarunos goes on.*"

Still in fox form, she stopped in mid-step and screamed. "No. It cannot be."

Vulpine had run ahead of her. Now he turned and bounded back. "What?"

"The child has been conceived."

The fog of the change rose from the ground, surrounded Katarina-the-fox, faded, and left her once again in human form. "What now?" she demanded of Rhonal.

"*I wait. My time will come again.*"

"No. I've waited long enough. Mirabella will not win."

"*She and Alamonar have already won.*"

"Christian will be mine," Katarina raged. But Rhonal did not answer. She curled her hands into fists. "Fine. I do not need you. I will take care of Mirabella myself."

"Katarina?" Vulpine stood before her in human shape.

She forced herself to take a calming breath. "Rhonal has forsaken us."

He reached toward her, but she stepped back. "Then we return to the castle?"

"Of course not," she snapped. "They all must die."

"Don't be a fool. Without Rhonal you cannot stand against the Goddess Anete and Mirabella."

Katarina smiled. "I have learned much from him." She lifted her hand and admired her

dagger-sharp nails. "Just a scratch. It is all that is needed. Then there will be no Mirabella, and there will be no child." She looked at him. "You will still take me to them."

"And what will my reward be for doing so?"

She narrowed her eyes. "Reward? I will let you live."

"I desire more." Their gazes locked, but Vulpine did not look away.

"More than your life?" She moved to him and caressed his chest with the tips of her fingernails, watched his eyes as she did. When he did not flinch or pull back, she laughed. "Oh, Vulpine, you never cease to please me. I see it now. I've been a fool to desire Christian. You are the mate for me. We will take care of him and Mirabella, and then..."

It was his turn to laugh. "You think I trust your sudden change of heart."

Her smile faded.

"But I care not." He went on. "We were meant to be together. Christian will bore you once you've beaten your rival and taken him to your bed. It is all about besting Mirabella, not about his love."

Katarina shrugged. "Believe what you wish. You will guide me to them?"

"I will, but we will not kill her and the child." He lifted his hand to stop her protests. "We will use the child to control Alamonar as we planned all along."

"But the prophecy?"

Vulpine snorted. "We will change it. The citizens too know of the child. They are ripe to follow his words. We will place the words in his mouth. With Mirabella imprisoned and Christian and the others dead, who will stop us?"

"There is the Goddess."

"As you said, you have learned much from Rhonal. Drawing upon the dark magic, we can surely bind the hands of one goddess."

"We will hold the child as hostage," Katarina said. "They will tread lightly as long as she thinks there is chance for the child to be saved." Katarina smiled. "It is a good plan. Now take me to them."

Vulpine nodded. He knew she would try to spare Christian, but that would not happen. His rival would be dead before they left the Goddess' glade.

Chapter Fourteen

A DIM LIGHT again filled the glade, it brightened by the moment. Brianna heard a muffled laugh and looked toward the willow. Mirabella and Christian came from within it, their fingers linked. They shared a warm look and caress and then Mirabella walked to the fallen tree. The ground squirrel came around it. She picked up the small creature and looked into its eyes.

"Rhonal has been leashed once again by the other gods and goddesses." She turned to look at the others, pressed her hand against her stomach. "The Child of Prophecy will be born."

"What of Katarina?" Mason said.

Mirabella frowned. "I cannot sense her."

"Without Rhonal, she'll give it up," Brianna said. "Won't she?"

Christian came to Mirabella and placed his hands on her bare shoulders. "Hate for Mirabella consumes Katarina. She is not one to accept defeat."

Mirabella sat the groundhog upon the tree. Its green eyes looked at each of them, and then it bobbed its head, ran the length of the trunk, and jumped down.

Brianna shivered. "Can we get dressed now?"

"Once we leave the glade," Mirabella said. She took Christian's hand. "Let's go home."

Outside the glade, beneath a full sun, they dressed again. Brianna looked around. She saw nothing to fear, but the shivers would not leave her

body.

"What is it my love?" Mason said.

"I just can't get warm. I hope I'm not catching a cold bug."

He rubbed her arms briskly and then leaned forward to whisper into her ear. "If we were alone, I could get you hot."

Her face heated. "Yes, you could," she said and smiled, but the unease that itched the back of her neck did not go away.

She turned to Mirabella. "How soon can Mason and I go back to our world?"

"With Mason's power unblocked, I can send you back now if you like."

The words surprised her. She looked into Mirabella's face. "I'll never see you again, will I?"

"Not in a physical form, but I will watch over you," Mirabella said.

"And the child? He's like my cousin or something." Her vision blurred and a tear slipped down her cheek.

Christian crossed to her and captured the tear with his fingertip. "We are all related by blood, for we are all children of the gods and goddesses."

"I like that, although I don't really care for Katarina as a distant sister."

"And I don't care for you either." Katarina raced toward Mirabella with arms outstretched, her fingers extended like claws.

"No," Vulpine screamed. "You are to kill the others, but the child must live."

"I changed my mind." Her words were the screech of a raptor as it dove upon its prey.

Brianna saw Mason lunge for Vulpine. He tackled the man's knees and they both fell to the

ground. They rolled. The sounds of heavy breathing, harsh curses, and connecting blows filled the clearing.

Gnaw snarled and growled as she danced around the struggle, then she darted in to sink her teeth into Vulpine's right leg. The man screamed and kicked out. Gnaw yelped. The sound broke Brianna's paralysis. Rage filled her. She saw a thick limb and picked it up. All she needed was a clear shot at Vulpine's head. Behind her, she heard a woman's gurgled scream and whirled. Christian had his hands around Katarina's throat. Bloody rivulets ran down each side of his cheeks. Mirabella lay still behind them.

"Bitch," he said. "Bitch."

Katarina clawed at his hands, but he continued his death grip. Katarina went limp, and still he did not release her.

"Christian," Brianna said. "Christian, you can let go now."

He looked up and their gazes met. His eyes were wild and vacant. Afraid to touch him, she simply held his look. He blinked and then, with a harsh intake of breath, jerked his hands back from Katarina's neck. She dropped like a broken doll and sprawled at his feet. He stared at her body and a stricken look crossed his face.

Brianna licked her lips and then touched his arm. "She can't hurt anybody anymore."

With a jerky motion, he turned to Mirabella and knelt beside her. He gathered her into his arms, and Brianna saw the raw gash and swollen lump at the side of Mirabella's head.

Mirabella moaned and opened her eyes. She lifted a hand to touch the bloody gashes along

Christian's cheek.

"Don't cry, my love," she whispered. "My head feels as if it will burst, but I will live."

Brianna became aware of the quiet behind her. She turned. Vulpine and Mason had separated. Both dripped blood and panted. The two men, still as rocks, stared at each other. A silent message seemed to pass between them, and then Vulpine looked at Katarina's still form. A wounded-soul cry erupted from him as he turned and ran into the trees. Gnaw yipped, but Mason grabbed the wolf pup by her neck-ridge. "Let him go."

"Mason?" Brianna said.

"I owed him for yours' and Christian's release. The debt is paid."

"By-the Goddess, no." Mirabella's scream had them running to her.

Christian lay stretched upon the ground, his breathing shallow and his eyes dull. The scratches along his cheek had become a sickly brownish-green.

"Her fingernails were poisoned," Mirabella said. "He dies."

"No," Brianna said. "Do something. Magik. Herbs. Something."

"It is a dark poison. If I had time...but there is none." Tears ran down her cheeks. "No, my love, no. Our child needs its father."

Christian's eyes focused. He lifted his hand to touch her cheek and then rested it against her stomach.

Brianna became aware of a sweet scent of flowers and grass. She turned and looked behind them. A woman encased in a shroud of white light floated toward them. Her eyes were dark, without

pupils, and filled with stars.

"Goddess, save him," Mirabella said.

A look of sorrow crossed the woman's face. Her lips did not move, but her words flowed into Brianna's mind. "I cannot."

"What do you mean, you can't?" Brianna said. "You're a goddess."

"I was given leeway to aid as long as Rhonal was a threat, but that is no longer true..."

"But he caused this," Brianna said. "This is his poison."

The Goddess shook her head. "I can do nothing."

"What are you doing?" Brianna heard Mason say. She turned back to him. Mirabella had stood. She moved to Katarina and picked up a limp hand.

"Daughter, stop," the Goddess said. "It is not the answer."

"I do not wish to live without him. You cannot bring him back, so I will join him in death. We will wait until we can be together again in a new life."

"What of the child? What of all of Alamonar?" The Goddess said.

Mirabella bowed her head. Her body shook.

"My love." The low words came from Christian.

Mirabella rushed to him.

"Love our child," he said. "Promise me."

Mirabella looked away.

"Promise me," Christian said, his hand grasping hers.

She looked into his eyes. "I will love our child as I love you," she said at last. His hand fell back to his side, and his eyes closed.

Aftermath

Tears of disbelief filled Brianna's eyes, ran down her cheeks. With a cry, she turned to Mason and he gathered her into his arms. Gnaw whined and pressed against Brianna's legs. This wasn't supposed to happen. This wasn't a happily-ever-after moment.

She felt warmth enter her arm. The Goddess' hand lay upon it. "It is time for you to go home."

"But Mirabella."

"Time and the coming child will heal her."

Brianna looked to the sobbing woman. It didn't seem right to leave her, but there was nothing she or Mason could do or say. She looked at Mason and he nodded. "Okay. What do we do?"

The Goddess smiled. "I will do it all." She ran her fingertips above Brianna's eyes and then did the same to Mason's. "You will sleep, and when you awake, you will be home."

"Gnaw. Don't forget Gnaw," Brianna said. The last thing she saw before sleep claimed her was the Goddess' smile.

*****

With eyes closed, Brianna stretched. She became aware of an arm around her waist and a warm body pressed against her. Something soft tickled her cheek. Her eyes opened to a pair of gold ones staring back.

"Gnaw," she said and scratched behind the wolf pup's ear. Then it all washed over her. Mirabella. Christian's death. She sat up. She was in a large four-poster bed. Mason lay beside her. It wasn't her bedroom, so it must be his.

They were home.

Mason opened his eyes. She saw the moment realization came to him. He pulled her close. Emotions warred within her. She was home. Her visit to Alamonar had left her with pain, but it had also brought her love, but Mirabella?

Mason released her and stood. "We are to go to my art gallery."

"What?"

He didn't answer her, just circled to her side of the bed and held out his hand.

She let him pull her to her feet. He led her from the room, with Gnaw following, down a flight of stairs and into the small art gallery.

"I don't get it," Brianna said.

Mason pulled her deeper into the room. "I understand. Look," he said.

There were six new paintings on the walls. There was the first of Mirabella in the Goddesses' glade, but then there was a next. It showed Mirabella with a child being breast-fed. The next showed Mirabella walking in the woods, holding the hand of a little boy. In the third, Mirabella stood with a young man who towered above her. The fourth showed the same young man at a wedding, a woman looking into his eyes adoringly. The fifth painting was of the man and woman upon twin thrones, and the last and final painting showed a contented town with people going about their lives.

Brianna felt tears fill her eyes, but they were tears of peace and joy. She linked her fingers with Mason's and, with Gnaw leading, they walked from the room.

RAINBOW RAINDROPS

Rainbow Raindrops

A gust of wind drove rain beneath the hood of my jacket and into my eyes. "What the hell am I doing?"

I ducked into the shadowed alcove of the City Museum. Sunlight broke from behind a dark cloud and bathed the street in light. The rain continued to stream and I looked through a curtain of tear-shaped rainbows. Rainbow raindrops.

I closed my eyes and again felt Grandpa's callused hand in mine. I smelled his Aqua Velva as we walked in the soft rain, our hands swinging in-time to his humming of the Tennessee Waltz. "Ready, Princess Annabelle. One...two...three...now turn, and turn..."

His hand lifted mine high over my head, and I turned, around and around, in the misty wetness, dancing among the rainbow raindrops, feeling them clinging to my eyelashes and running unheeded down my cheeks.

"Grandpa," I whispered and for a moment I almost remembered how to smile again.

"You coming in, Miss?"

The words came from behind me.

I blinked my eyes, turned. "What?"

A security guard had opened the door to the museum. "You're blocking the door. Are you coming in?"

"Yes, I guess I am."

Inside, I dropped the hood of my jacket back.

Aftermath

I saw the guard glance at my green turban and then look quickly away. I pushed by him without a word and headed for the wall of French Impressionists at the far back.

In front of the muted colors of a Monet, I hugged my stomach and blinked back tears. Grandpa was gone, grandma, too, and that happy little girl was nothing but a bitter memory. When I'd danced among the rainbow raindrops, I'd believed in happily ever after – a blue-and-yellow house with a white picket fence, a handsome husband, and two brown-eyed kids; a boy and a girl.

What a crock. My caustic laugh caused a middle-aged man and woman to stare at me, and I glared back until they looked away and hurried down the hallway.

I wandered on, stopped to look into a glass case.

My wavering reflection stared back at me. I reached to touch the green turban. My eyes were like sunken holes, so dark were the circles that surrounded them. I knew the rest of my body resembled a walking cadaver. I could sure wear a bikini now. I'd finally lost those stubborn ten pounds of chubby fat that had always clung to my stomach and thighs. Now that's a diet you never read about in the women's magazines – the chemotherapy plan. I laughed again and looked around to see if anybody else wanted to stare at me, but I was alone in the dim room.

I really didn't like the new, bitter me, but it seemed impossible to change, and why should I? I was dying.

I clamped my lips together, held back the scream that always seemed so close to eruption. I

Aftermath

was only twenty-five. Women weren't supposed to get ovarian cancer and die at twenty-five. I hugged my stomach again, felt the emptiness.

A woman entered the room. She looked at me, and I ducked behind a tall display case. I didn't want her to see the tears that streaked my cheeks. When I looked again, she was gone.

I wandered into another room.

Among suits of armor and Renaissance shields, I could see a young boy in a dark three-piece suit. He hopped from one stream of slanting sunlight to another. His cheeks were rosy with life and, for a moment, I hated him. Then he glanced at me and I could see that his blue eyes were wide with pain. I turned awa. I didn't want to know what had left such anguish there.

I walked back into the room of French Impressionist paintings.

A young, black, and very pregnant girl leaned against a marble column in the room's center. Her hands caressed her bulging stomach as she stared into nothingness. I moved quickly by her.

Next to the museum's gift room was a coffee shop. Inside, dry, ventilated air reeked of scorched coffee and stale grease. My legs trembled as I headed toward a far table beneath the shop's one window. I plopped into a hard-bottomed chair and winced. No padding there anymore. A phantom strand of hair tickled my cheek and I brushed at it, even though I knew it wasn't really there. I felt sick and needed a drink of water but was afraid to stand.

"You can see me, can't you," a voice asked.

I glanced up. It was the woman I'd glimpsed earlier. Where had she come from? I hadn't seen her come through the door. She was stuffed into an

azure, polyester two-piece pants suit. Her blonde hair looked like it was lacquered in place and two bright-pink circles of blush decorated her cheeks.

Go away, I wanted to say, but instead asked, "What do you mean."

Her glossy carmine lips spread in a big smile. "You can see me."

I rubbed at the back of my neck. "I'd like to be alone."

She plopped down in the chair across from me. "But why?" she said and then slapped the table top.

"I've got it. You're dying." She glanced at my turban. "The big 'C', right?"

I glared at her silence.

You know, cancer," she added.

I looked around for someone to summon, a pest exterminator with a full knowledge of poisons preferably. "Leave me alone."

"That's gotta be it. You've got a leg in both worlds. That's why you can see me."

I started to risk standing, but then she stood, her ample bosom rising right through the wood of the table. With a small squeal, I dropped back into my chair. "How'd you do that?"

She glanced down. "Sorry. I guess that wasn't the best way to spill the beans." She held out her chubby hand. "I'm Trudy Mills, and I'm dead."

Without thought, I reached out to shake her hand. There was a tingle of cold as mine passed right through hers.

"Oh, my God." I glanced around wildly; but other than the bored-looking young man behind the counter, we were alone. "Get away from me," I yelled and surged to my feet.

The young man bolted from behind the counter and hurried to me. "Is there a problem?" "Make her get away from my table," I said.

Trudy shook her head at me in a clear warning.

"Who, lady?"

"Her." I pointed toward Trudy. "Can't you see her?"

He took a step back from me. "Maybe I'd just better get security..."

"No, wait. Can't you tale a joke? Of course there isn't anyone there. You just looked so bored..."

He turned away. "Can I get you anything?"

Trudy's laughter should have drowned out my answer of, "A glass of ice water, please."

He nodded and walked away.

When Trudy had herself under control, she said. "Most times the living can't see us. It's because you've got one foot in the grave that you can."

"Us?" I said. "There are more of you?"

She nodded. "What's your name, sweetie?"

"Annabel Lee."

"A beautiful name." She smiled. "It was many and many a year ago, " she recited, her eyes half-closed. "In a kingdom by the sea. That a maiden there lived whom you may know by the name of Annabel Lee."

My mouth must have dropped open, because she opened her eyes wide and frowned at me.

"What? You don't think that someone like me could know poetry?"

"I..."

"Well, for your information, I love Poe, and I can't wait to meet him. I can do the whole Raven.

You want to hear it?"

"No, " I said and leaned back.

"Just as well. The kid's coming with your water. His name's Chuck. He's been working here about a month."

The young man handed me the glass. "It's starting to really come down outside. You want me

to call you a cab?"

"No, I think I'll stay a little longer."

He shrugged his shoulders and walked away. "Suit yourself."

I heard a low whistle and faced Trudy.

"Favor blondes myself, but his butt ain't half bad, is it?"

I couldn't get words to form, so simply nodded.

"Don't look so scared. I'm not going to bite you. I'm a ghost, not a vampire, but I guess I could be called the walking dead though. Right?" Looking very pleased with herself, she hooted a nerve-jangling laugh.

"The others?" I said forcing my lips to smile.

Trudy stood. "Let's go meet them." She touched my arm and I felt that cold tingle again.

I shook my head. "I don't think so."

Trudy reached toward me. "You gotta. How else are you going to set us free?"

"Me? What can I do? I'm not a priest. I haven't even been in church for months."

"But you can see us. All you have to do is listen." She looked over my shoulder. "Look, here comes Jonathan."

I turned in my chair. It was the little boy with the sad eyes I'd seen earlier.

"It's okay, Johnny, she can see us," Trudy said and motioned him forward. He came to stand beside Trudy. His eyes studied his toes and a small, shy smile curved his lips. I noticed the color I'd seen earlier on his cheeks. It wasn't good health, but a garish pink blush.

"She's gonna help."

The boy's head jerked up. An expression of hope filled his brown eyes and I swallowed my words of denial.

"You are? You're going to set us free?" Without waiting for my answer, he turned and ran through the nearest wall. "Wait 'til I tell the others."

I faced Trudy, angry at being manipulated, but she just smiled. "Johnny's been here thirty-five years. You can't blame him for being excited."

"Thirty-five years? But how...?"

"His mommy only turned for a minute. He was on a merry-go-round, but that was all it took for some sicko to lure him away."

"I don't get it. Why are you all stuck here?"

"We got killed all of a sudden, and none of us got the chance to say what the one thing was that had made us so happy to be alive."

"That's it? I let you tell me what that was, and you're out of here?"

Trudy winked at me. "That's it."

"But why here? And why me?"

"I already told you why, and the here? What better place for old relics to wait, because that's what we all are, no matter our ages, old relics from years gone by."

"How long have you been here?"

"Me?" Trudy turned and walked to the door and, wanting an answer, I stood and followed. "Not

long. Only twenty-two years."

"But...." I motioned towards her polyester pants suit.

She laughed. "It's my step-daughter's revenge. I told her daddy I caught her smoking. She knew I hated polyester anything. And when you go unexpected like, you don't get to pick out what you're buried in."

"How did it happen?"

The smile fled. "Too much booze and too little brains."

Trudy led me to the amphitheater where the museum held its public lectures. Every seat was taken.

"Oh, my God," I whispered.

"Hey, everyone," Trudy called. "This is Annabel Lee. She's come to listen to us."

I'd never been applauded by two hundred ghosts before and, surprisingly, I didn't faint.

Trudy turned to me. "Where do you want to start?"

I saw the pregnant young black woman I'd seen earlier, leaning against the door. "When did she die?"

"That's Chantel. She's been here thirty-two years."

"How?"

"She fell down the stairs. She was arguing with her mom. Her mom didn't like that the baby's daddy was white."

"I'll start with her."

"Chantel," Trudy called. "You're first."

Chantel came and stood before me. She clasped her hands on top of her stomach and, looking me straight in the eyes, said, "My happiest

day? It was when Darryl came home. My Darryl, he was n the Navy. He didn't even know about the baby." She caressed her stomach. "He took one look at me, and then he said, 'I love you, Chantel. Will you be my wife?'"

I squinted against a sudden glare. A white light formed in back of the young woman and, as the last word left her lips, the light surged forward, surrounded her in a golden shroud. It flared like an incandescent torch, and then it and Chantel were gone.

Trudy touched my arm. "Who's next?"

I pointed at Jonathan. The little boy whooped and sprang toward me.

I stayed that night until I was asked to leave, and came back the next day as soon as the doors opened. I stayed all that day, and the next, and the next. I knew the people at the museum thought I was crazy, but I didn't care. And yes, listening took a lot out of me. Sometimes I was so wrung out I could barely stumble home. I don't know when I stopped being afraid to die. One morning-I just wasn't.

It was Monday of the third week when I walked into the amphitheater and stopped in confusion. "Trudy, what's going on?"

"What do you mean?"

"I can see through you, all of you. Is this some kind of ghost trick?"

To my surprise, Trudy's face lit with a joyous smile. "My God, is that true? You're having a hard time seeing us?"

"What are you doing different?"

"Oh, Annabel, it's not us. It's you. Don't you

see? You're getting well. You're going back to the world of the living. You're not going to die."

I had felt better in the past week. "Trudy, you're fading." I felt the cold tingle of her hand brush my arm.

"It's okay. The rest of us can wait a little longer."

"No. I can still see you a little. Let's do it. You first. What has been your happiest day?"

"Them first."

I could no longer see her eyes and her face was just a soft blur.

One by one they glided toward me, telling me of their happiest days, until the last flared away. I turned around to smile my triumph at Trudy, but the amphitheater looked empty. "Trudy. Trudy. Dear God, Trudy, where are you?" Then I saw her, just a faint ripple of azure blue before me. "Tell me," I said. "Tell me."

"Today," she said, her voice the crackle of dried leaves. "Right now."

Then she too was gone.

I sat for a while in the total silence and then I left the museum. Outside, the rain fell. Behind each drop was a wash of bright sun, and I saw them, my rainbow raindrops.

With a small laugh, I raced out into the downpour and, humming the Tennessee Waltz, I began to dance, a dance of life.

THE GOLDEN AVATAR
A STORY OF DARADAWN

The Golden Avatar
A story of Daradawn

Part One

Wind whipped the reed boat; water flooded the deck with each side-to-side plunge. It scaled a wave, plummeted, shuddered with the force of its landing.

The lone survivor moaned as he surfaced into consciousness. He licked his dry lips. "Please, let me come to you now."

"No, Dahlabar, you will not die, for I have need of you."

It was the same voice that had spoken to him in his dreams, and for a moment he thought he still slept, but a slap of frigid sea-spray against his cheeks told him otherwise. With the aid of the boat's trembling sides, he pulled himself to his knees. He blinked his swollen eyes, stared across the rolling expanse of gray. Lightning slashed cross the darkening sky.

"What more must I give you?" he shouted into the gusting wind. "My brethren are gone, my ship destroyed."

"Your path unfolds, my son. Now sleep."

Lethargy bent his knees.

"I obey, Goddess." He slipped to the deck, sank once again into unconsciousness.

*****

A loud screech pierced his ears and Dahlabar snapped his eyes open. What manner of beast cried so?

A score of black-and-white birds the likes he'd

never seen before soared above him. What are they and where am I?

Thoughts flooded over him, the journey to fish, his five friends and the storm that dropped from the sky, fast and furious. How many days had passed since the sea had swallowed his brethren one by one? Three? Seven?

He pulled himself to his feet. Water spread before him, a brilliant blue carpet.

The boat rode soft swells, pushed onward by the wind's hand. He shaded his eyes. Dark fingers stretched across the horizon. Land. But whose? "What you will Goddess, I accept." He leaned against the side of the vessel and watched the shore grow larger.

The sea flowed toward a cove. Before him, waves surged over a reef. He held his breath as the boat rode high, then released it in a relieved gust as he crossed and settled back into the water.

Inside the inlet, the water calmed to a mirroring sheen. On the land, movement caught his eye. People ran down a length of beach, pointed, their panicked cries reached his ears, but he could not make out their words.

"Dahlabar, save the girl." The words formed in his head.

He saw her then, a small form that floundered in the waves. Without thought, he dove. With three strong strokes, he was beside her. Treading water, he reached out.

The girl screamed, "dark devil," and slapped at his hands.

The sea flooded his mouth and nose, and he coughed and spit. Then the child's eyes opened wide and all struggle left her body. He laced his

fingers in her hair as she went under.

One arm around her waist, he towed her toward shore. His feet struck sand and he stood with the child in his arms. On trembling legs, he stumbled forward. People rushed toward him with strangled cries. Their pale faces blurred as they pulled the child from his arms. Questions were thrown at him. He understood their words but, as he started to speak, darkness edged his vision and swallowed him.

✳✳✳✳✳

"Whore of Satan." The slap cracked in the small cottage. The woman stumbled back, blood dripped from the corner of her mouth. The man lifted his hand again, reeled as he overbalanced. His ale-laden breath billowed into the woman's face and she gagged.

"Kill it," the man ordered and pointed to the tiny, swaddled form. "Before I kill it and you." He turned, bounced off a table, and careened toward the door. "Be it not here when I return." The door slammed behind him.

The woman grabbed her stomach and sank to her knees. What had she done to birth this daughter of Satan? Pain gripped her. She stood and walked to the baby. With a sob, she picked up a pillow. The child's eyes, one blue and one brown, opened and stared up at her. The woman cried out and stepped back. Dropping the pillow, she made the holy sign upon her breasts. "Remove your gaze from me, devil child."

The baby began to wail and the woman's breast milk flowed in response. "Dear God, what am I to do? He will kill you." She turned to stare out the window. "You are but a babe. Perhaps the holy

fathers can help drive away the evilness before it is too late."

She wrapped the child in a warm blanket and, smothering her own sobs of fear and guilt, she hurried out the door.

At the top step of the temple of Ogdah, she listened. From inside came a voice raised in prayer. Avoiding her daughter's eyes, she kissed the babe's head and laid her gently down. "Go with God," she whispered, then turned and ran.

Inside the temple Father Milo lifted his head and stared at the stained glass rendering of his god washing a child's feet. He felt nothing looking into those soulful dark eyes, and his heart sank in despair. When had he lost his faith? When had the praying and hymn singing become only a day-to-day monotony?

He dropped to his knees before the carved alabaster alter. "Please, please." Silence rang in the temple that was as empty as his heart. Tears blurring his vision, he stood and walked to the double doors.

After the dimness of the holy chamber, the sun blinded him. He blinked his eyes, stepped forward. A voice rang in his head. *"Look down."*

"What?" he murmured. He glanced around, but the street was empty. "Who are you? I heard your voice? Come forward."

"Guard the child." The voice floated into his head again.

Father Milo closed his eyes. "Is that you, my god?" No answer came. He felt compelled to look down, spotted something on the stone steps. "A child?"

Holding the baby against his heart, his gaze

swept the street, but not a soul stirred. "Do you give unto me a child?"

Tears slipped down his cheeks as he walked back into the temple. Before the altar, he lifted the babe with hands that trembled. "I will protect your gift with my life. This I pledge." He heard footsteps and turned. A group of priests entered.

"What do you have, Brother Milo?" They circled him.

"A gift and a message from our god." He smiled at the picture portrayed in stained glass. "I had a crisis of faith, and this was my answer." The baby in his arms stirred and let out a loud wail.

"Let us view this gift," a priest demanded.

Milo pulled the blanket away from the child so all could look upon her face.

"Oh, what a beauty. A little angel."

The baby opened her eyes. A frozen stillness descended on the group of clerics, followed by panicked gasps and cries. The priests stumbled back, made warding signs.

"What have you done?" one demanded. "Our temple is cursed."

"Take it back to where you found it! It cannot stay among us."

Father Milo picked up the now screaming infant and held her against his chest. "I cannot. I have made a vow. Our god brought her to us. She cannot be evil."

"Look at her eyes. Darkness lies within her," a priest cried.

"She is an innocent," Father Milo said. "We can keep the evil from her. That is why she has been brought to us. We can..."

They turned their backs on him.

"Remove her from our sight," one ordered. "We will call for a meeting this night. The High Father will decide."

Milo jostled the baby in his arms. He had made a vow, but if the High Father overrode him, the child would be taken. Hot blood flooded his cheeks. No. He would not let it happen. Glaring, he pushed through them and headed toward the temple doors.

*****

The bells shrilled, their strident call. Father Milo smiled bitterly. They had wasted no time. His meager belongings lay on his cot wrapped in a tight bundle. He still wore his brown robe but, if things went as he feared, it too would be left behind. It was by the grace of his god he still had the tunic and trousers he had worn when he first crossed the Temple of Ogdah's threshold. They would serve him well now.

The bells had awakened the baby, but she looked into his face in silence as he picked her up and cradled her in his arms.

In the grounds before the monastery doors, a strange sight befell him. Holding the baby close, he looked across a crowd of liveried soldiers and guards. The king's herald stood heads above a circle of priests.

"He comes," a voice cried, and the crowd parted before him. He walked the aisle. Raised angry voices came to him.

"We will not," he heard the High Father say. "He is a heathen and fornicates with the dark god."

Father Milo quickened his steps. A guard stepped back to let the priest and child enter the circle. King Frederick stood before the High Father,

but it was the man who stood by the king's side that made Father Milo gasp. He was black as a moonless night.

As the priest approached, all gazes turned to him and then dropped to the child he carried.

"You will obey me, High Father," the king said. He pointed to the man. "He saved my daughter's life. I have made a promise, and anything he wishes he shall have. All he asks is to serve in the temple." He motioned. "Come forward, Dahlabar."

The priests drew back as the man stepped forward. "I follow the Goddess' path and she has led me to you," he said.

"Goddess?" the High Father sputtered. "There is no Goddess, only the true God."

King Frederick raised his hand. "Enough. He will remain among you for as long as he wishes. That is my command." He turned to Dahlabar. "This is what you ask of me?"

"It is."

"So be it." King Frederick mounted his horse and, flanked by his royal guards, rode away.

A stilted hush followed the king's retreat. Then Milo watched a crafty look spread across the High Father's face. "Bring the child here," he snapped with a hard glare.

Unease crawling along his spine, Milo stepped forward.

"I obey my king," the High Father said in a spiteful voice. "You," he pointed at Dahlabar, "will take and care for this child. It will be your only duty among us."

"But, Holy Father..." Milo began.

"Silence," the High Father said, his voice harsh. "It is only right that one of Satan's children

care for the other." He glared harder at the young priest. "You have brought this evil among us, but our god in his wisdom has also brought to us a solution." He turned back to Dahlabar. "There is a cottage in back of the temple. Take the baby. I do not wish to look upon either of you again." He turned on his heels and strode away from them.

Dahlabar stepped forward and held out his hands, but Father Milo hesitated, clutched the child to his heart.

"I understand," the black man said, "but it is her path. You have fulfilled your part. Now it is my turn. Do not fear. I will love and care for her as the Goddess wills."

With a sigh tinged with relief, Milo released the baby into Dahlabar's arms. He thought of the wrapped bundle he had left on the cot. His decision had been made as he stared into the High Father's sharp eyes. This life was not for him and now he could leave with an easy heart, knowing the child would be cared for. "I will show you the cottage."

Dahlabar followed the priest to the cottage and stepped inside. He stared around the single small room. It was cold and empty. He looked down into the baby's eyes.

"We will fill it with warmth. You are Thea, Nature's Child. The Goddess has named you so."

And Thea smiled at his words.

Part Two

"Thea, gather your belongings," Dahlabar said, as he came through the cottage door.

She looked up from the book she read. "What is it, poppa-Dah?"

She watched him smile at her name for him. When she was a baby, she had not been able to say Dahlabar, but now it was the term of love she always chose.

"It is time we moved beyond these walls."

Thea looked around. For the past six years this had been their home. Why were they to leave now? Surely the sour-faced priests who avoided her eyes like donkey dung would not want them in the monastery. Had the High Father at last won his fight with the King? Were they being thrown from their home? "Where do we go, poppa-Dah?"

"The woodcutter and his wife have gone to be with the Goddess. The king has granted their cottage in the deep woods to us." He walked to the far wall and picked up a stack of books from the crude table he'd built. "It is time for you to learn more of the Goddess' world."

A thrill knotted her stomach. "What am I to take?"

He looked around. "Everything."

Not a soul stirred as the pony pulled the loaded cart across the grounds. As they exited the gates, Thea looked back. She left the only home she'd known, but all she felt was a surge of happy anticipation for what lay ahead.

*****

Thea wiped sweat from her forehead, sat back on her heels and looked around. The settling in was at last finished. The cottage was bigger than the one they'd left behind, with thick walls and shutters that would block frigid winds and rain. She even had her own place above in the loft.

Their meager furnishings, added to those of the now gone couple, filled the rooms with comfort. Braided rugs in front of the hearth and table added circles of color. Drying herbs, suspended in corners, wrapped the area in scents of lavender, thyme and lemon basil. Tomorrow she would look for mint to join with them.

From outside she heard the whack and crack as Dahlabar chopped wood. She had teased him earlier about cutting enough to last them through the winter in one day. And he had laughed and called her a lazy bumpkin, telling her to get back to work.

A lazy bumpkin, indeed, she thought with a sniff. I will show him. She planned to make their first meal in their new home a splendid one. Already a fire burned high in the hearth. Sliced potatoes, carrots and onions waited for water in the round pot hanging above the flames. Along with the stew she would serve cheese, soft slices of crushed-wheat bread, and cold, clear water from the well. Happiness made her feet itch and, unable to remain still, she stood and danced around the room, singing the rhyme poppa-Dah used to send her to sleep for as far back as she could remember.

"You are a butterfly," Dahlabar said from behind her, and she spun with a laugh.

"No, not a butterfly, poppa-Dah, but a warble-bird, delighted in its own little nest."

"Earlier I saw some ripe juice berries," he said.

They would be wonderful. I will..."

"No, daughter, I will fetch them. Unless you wish a ruined stew."

Thea smiled. Her poppa-Dah could coax a pile of sand to grow and blossom, but a simple meal was beyond him. "Give me two fingers of time. Then all will be ready," she said.

Dahlabar grinned. "You have learned your lessons well."

Each morning they spent time on her learning. The method of plotting the day's passing had been one of her first. She held up her hand. "One hand spread three times, held up to the heavens and spaced thumb to little finger, make up the first part of the day," she recited. "And then three more make up the waning into night. The time between each hand is broken into finger widths."

Dahlabar nodded. "In two fingers, but I will hope for less. Already my stomach grumbles." He turned and walked from the cottage.

*****

Time passed. Snow came, departed, followed by spring's first flowers and summer's warm sun.

One bright morning, bird song woke Dahlabar and he knew without looking that he was alone. The cottage always felt empty when Thea was not around. The large woven basket kept by the door was gone. His daughter gathered herbs.

He rose and broke his fast with cheese and bread. When three fingers passed and Thea did not return, unease moved him to the cottage door.

The sun rode high in a crystalline-blue sky. He chanted a prayer to the Goddess, thanked her for her blessings as he moved beneath the coolness of the forest's trees.

Thea was not at the first three places he looked and his unease grew. The woods held no large predators, but a broken leg could fell one with the same swiftness as a pack of wolves.

He heard her voice before he saw her.

She spoke gently, coaxing. "Come, little one. Let me see."

Dahlabar stopped beside the trunk of a large oak. On her knees in the sun-dappled clearing, Thea spoke to a spiky, green bush. As he watched, a small rabbit came from its concealment. It moved toward her with a limping hop. His daughter cocked her head. "A thorn, I see. Which foot?"

The rabbit held out its right front paw.

Thea turned it over. "And it's gone nasty, too. No wonder it hurts you."

He watched her work the thorn free and then reach into the pocket of her gown and pull out a leaf-wrapped bundle. "This will make it well."

She undid the leaves and smeared a thick layer of green salve on the rabbit's foot. The rabbit laid its head on her knee.

"You are quite welcome," Thea said.

Dahlabar bowed his head. "Blessed Goddess, you have gifted my daughter with much. For this I thank you." When he looked up, the rabbit was gone. Thea sat, smiling into the sky. "Daughter?"

"Poppa-Dah, I did not hear you."

"The rabbit...you understood its words?" He knew the answer, but asked anyway.

"Yes, a hurt foot."

"You understand others?"

"I am a healer, poppa-Dah. A beautiful woman, haloed by light, came to me as I slept and told me so. She said she was The Mother to Us All, and that she gave me the way to understand the words of all creatures."

"When did this happen?"

"It came with the rebirth of the year," Thea said.

"I knew the Goddess had planned your path when she brought us together," Dahlabar said. "But I did not know what lay before you upon it."

Thea smiled. "I am happy it is so. Already I have spoken to a ram with curled horns from the now-capped mountains, and an eagle whose home is by the sea."

"There will be more, my daughter."

"And with each I will do my best."

Aftermath

Part Three

Thea hummed as she crushed the dried leaves of mint with the smooth rock. The sweet herb, seeped in simmering water, would help the fox kit's sour stomach. As her hands worked, her gaze drifted to the far wall with its rows of black slashes. She'd made the first mark when they'd been in the cottage the first nine sunrises. Now the wall was covered with the slashes. By poppa-Dah's count, today was the sixteenth celebration of her birth. Ten years they had been together in the cottage, and what wondrous creatures she had seen and healed. All thanks to the Goddess. She bowed her head and whispered her morning greeting. Dahlabar still snored behind the curtain that hid his sleeping chamber. She had aged, but time's hand did not seem to touch her poppa-Dah. Was that too by the Goddess' will?

She heard a soft snort and then a commanding whinny. What was that? A horse? They did not come often to her. Thea wiped her hands on her apron and moved to the cottage door.

It was a stallion, blinding white in the morning sun, rider-less and saddle-less. The horse tossed his head as she stared into his eyes. She reached to stroke its ears. "What do you wish from me?"

"*You are needed.*" The thought floated into her mind, and the horse turned from her.

Without question, Thea entered the cottage, gathered her herbs and salves and followed the stallion.

He led her into the forest, deeper than she

had ventured before.

The stallion entered a small clearing and in its center a still figure laid. A quick glance at the man's leg, twisted beneath him, told her it was broken. His face was pale, but his breathing and heartbeat were strong. The best she could hope to do was splint it, give him something for the pain, and get him back to the cottage. She found two straight limbs and, thanking the Goddess the man still slept, she straightened his leg, winced as he moaned. She splinted it and had tied the last knot when she felt him stir.

She looked up and met his eyes, stilled herself for the fear she would see there, but his brown gaze only held bewilderment.

"Who are you?" he said.

"I am Thea, daughter of Dahlabar."

"Thea," he repeated. He moved and then gasped.

"Don't," she said. "You have broken your leg."

"My leg." He rubbed at his forehead. "Now I remember. A bear chased me. I climbed the tree." He pointed to a tall oak. "And fell as I came down."

"Why did you not just run from it..."

He frowned at her. "I am fleet on my feet, but I cannot outrun a bear."

Thea flushed. "Of course not. Your horse could have..." She turned to point at the stallion, but it was gone.

"I don't have a horse. I was walking."

She looked around in surprise. "A stallion brought me to you."

The man struggled to sit up.

"If you must sit up, at least let me help you," she said. "But first take this." She handed him a

finger's width of dried poppy seeds. "It will lessen the pain." She watched in silence as he chewed the seeds. "I would know your name," she said as he swallowed.

The man flushed. "I apologize. I am Desmond, mage apprentice." He stared into her eyes. "I have not seen you among the other apprentices."

"I do not attend the Mage School," she said.

"You do not?" His voice was sharp with surprise. "But I feel the power surge from you. It surrounds you with a green aura. And your eyes..."

She looked away from him. "You do not fear my slightest glance?" Her face heated at the bitter tone of her words.

"No. I have read of such eyes. You have been blessed by the gods."

"Not the gods," she said with a smile. "The Goddess." She stood and reached down to him. "Are you ready to stand?"

The poppy seeds had done their job, but still Desmond gasped as together they got him up onto his feet. Thea felt her knees try to buckle as he leaned against her. "This will never do," she said.

She heard a soft snort and turned. The stallion stood across the clearing from them. "No horse?" she said.

"He is not mine."

Dahlabar came from the trees.

"Father," Thea said. "I am so glad to see you."

"The stallion brought me to you," her father said. "What has happened?"

"Desmond has broken his leg," she said. "He is from the Mage School."

Dahlabar came to Desmond's other side. "We

will get him up on the horse." He glanced at the darkening sky. "It is too late to take him to the school tonight. We will take him there in the morn."

Thea looked up in surprise. Where had the day gone? It had been morning when she'd left with the stallion.

It was a struggle but, with the Dahlabar's aid and the use of Desmond's good leg, they were able to get him up on the horse. Even so, the man's face was as white as the stallion by the time he was mounted.

Desmond grimaced as he laced his fingers in the stallion's mane.

Thea resisted the urge to pat his hand, somehow she knew Desmond would resent it. Instead she turned and walked from him. "The ride is not far."

They walked in silence beneath a canopy of trees. She walked at one side of the stallion's head and Dahlabar at the other. The shadows deepened and she began to fear that full darkness would descend before they made it to the cottage. The horse stumbled and Dahlabar reached to touch between its ears. "Careful, Goddess."

"You called the stallion Goddess?" Desmond's voice surprised her. She thought he'd drifted into sleep.

"I did," Dahlabar said.

"But it's a male."

"It is the Goddess." Dahlabar's voice held certainty.

Thea nodded in the darkness. Of course the stallion was She- Who- Is- the- Mother- to- Us-All. She turned and sought Desmond's pale face. Why had she been led to this mage apprentice? Yes, he

had broken his leg and needed aid, but she felt there was something more in the Goddess' plan.

She smiled at the thought of the Goddess choosing to take the form of a stallion and not a mare to make herself known in a physical presence.

The stallion butted her in the shoulder and she turned to stare into the horse's eyes. Amusement lurked there.

"You say I am riding upon the back of a goddess?" Desmond's voice jerked her attention back to him.

"She led me to you," Thea said. "If not you would still be lying on the ground." She recognized a lightning-struck tree. "We are almost home."

They entered the clearing and could see the cottage. Soft light filtered from the edges of the shutters and smoke floated from the chimney. She felt a surge of happiness.

Without prompting, the stallion stopped beside the stump Dahlabar used for splitting wood.

Thea rushed to Desmond's side, but was stopped by a slight shake of Dahlabar's head.

The young mage swung his good leg over the horse's back and slid onto the stump. She heard him gasp, but he remained upright, clutching the stallion's mane.

The stump was a good three axe lengths high. She wondered how he was going to complete the journey to the ground. He could break his other leg. He glanced at her and his face flushed. Still he just stood there. Was she the problem? Male pride, she thought with a disdainful sniff, then turned on her heels and walked toward the cottage. Behind her she heard voices, but she did not cease her quick pace.

Aftermath

She opened the cottage door and stopped short. Tears filled her eyes. A cake sat in the middle of the table. It tilted to the side and icing coated more of the trencher it rested in, but it was a cake in celebration of her birth. The thought that she was sixteen summers old today had skipped her mind. Fresh flowers, some in jugs, others tied into small nosegays, and still others woven into garlands, decorated the room. She breathed in their sweet perfume, almost unable to swallow around the lump in her throat. A wrapped package lay on her chair next to the table. She moved to it and picked it up.

"Open it," Dahlabar said.

She turned. He and Desmond stood just inside the doorway. She watched the young mage's glance sweep over the cottage.

"I have disrupted your birth celebration," he said.

"Maybe you are but another gift," she said, and then felt her face burn as the words left her lips. The mage smiled and hopped further into the room with Dahlabar's help. "No matter. I promise you another gift when I am able to return to you with it." Not meeting Desmond's eyes, Thea fumbled with the string that tied the package she still gripped. "Oh," she said, as she caught sight of the cornflower-blue fabric. "What is it?" She pushed the wrappings aside and pulled the gift free. It was a gown. She held it to her cheek. It was like rubbing against a fawn's skin. "But poppa-Dah, how? When...?" Her words trailed away.

Dahlabar smiled. "I have had sixteen summers to make it happen. I cannot give you much..."

"Don't," she said. "I have all I could ever want or need."

"Put it on," Dahlabar said. "We will wait."

She did not need to be urged twice. With a soft laugh, she turned and ran toward the loft ladder.

Her loft room was a haven for her, but just now she gave it but a cursory glance. She draped the blue gown across the bed and then slipped from the dress and apron she wore. Even with the new one waiting, she took time to hang the old upon the pegs protruding from the wall beam.

Thea shivered as the gown's soft folds slid down her body. She imagined it would be the same as a lover's touch. Such had been on her mind a lot lately, and her skin heated in response.

Her thoughts shifted to the young man below. He had nice hands and wonderful green eyes. They reminded her of the moss that coated the rocks by the stream. His reddish hair had surprised her. She had not known someone could have hair the same shade of a fox's fur. She ran her hands along her hips. The gown was beautiful and fit wonderfully. It was a bit tight in the bosom, but that had been a recent body change hidden by the shapelessness of her other gowns.

She placed her hand on the low, round neckline. It displayed much flesh. Had her father known of that feature of its design? She doubted it. She glanced down at the grass-stained toes of her boots peeking from beneath the gown's hem. It would have been nice to have slippers to match, but such things were not practical for woodland hikes.

Thea moved to her most treasured

possession, a narrow mirror almost as long as she was tall.

She had not asked where or how Dahlabar had gotten it, only laughed with delight as they had maneuvered it up the ladder into her room. She was not in the habit of gazing upon herself, but today was different.

She looked at the reflection staring back. What she saw was a young woman with sun-blonde hair, pulled back from an oval face, and plaited into one long braid whose banded end brushed a trim waist. Bright blue eye, fringed with dark lashes, glowed with excitement. Her skin was softly golden, like a peach's skin. She sighed as she touched a cheek pink with happiness; her skin would never be the milk white so favored by the court ladies. "But I've a different path before me," she murmured.

"Daughter, my stomach growls." Dahlabar's voice rose to her.

Smoothing the gown, she turned from the mirror. "I am coming, poppa-Dah."

Dahlabar stood at the ladder and, as her foot found the third rung, he grabbed her around the waist, pulled her from the ladder and swung her in a circle.

She laughed in delight as her head whirled, keeping time with the spinning room. "No more. I will be sick."

Dahlabar stopped and then walked to her chair and deposited her in it. He stepped back and bowed to her from the waist. "Tonight you are my princess. How may I serve you?" The twinkles in his eyes branded his subservient tone a lie.

She flicked her fingers toward him. "I desire cake, knave. And my goblet is empty of wine."

"I only live to please," Dahlabar said and turned toward their water jug.

"If my lady wishes, I will cut the cake," Desmond said, hobbling toward the table.

"Oh. No," she said starting to rise.

"Stay," Desmond ordered. "I am already here."

"Then at least sit down," she said and to the last chair.

"I'll not take my host's seat."

"Settle, young mage," Dahlabar said. "Tonight I serve."

"If you do not sit, then neither will I," Thea said and stood. Desmond's lips tightened, but she cocked at eyebrow at him. "It is my command," she added.

The young mage smiled and slid into the chair.

She and then held out her goblet. "Now, wine, knave." And then felt her eyes widen as red liquid poured from the pitcher's mouth. "But...I did but jest. Where...?"

"A celebration, is it not, daughter?" Dahlabar poured wine into Desmond's goblet and then into another. He raised his high. "Happy sixteenth birth anniversary," he said.

Desmond also lifted his goblet, and then the two men waited and watched until she lifted her wine to her mouth and sipped. It was sweet and tart at the same time, and coated her throat with warmth as she swallowed. The wine hit her empty stomach and the heat spread. "My," she said, fanning her face with her hand.

Yes, a good vintage," Desmond said after taking a long drink.

Dahlabar raised an eyebrow. "You drink wine often at the Mage School?"

The young man flushed, but instead of answering he took another drink.

Sensing his words to be only youthful boasting, Thea stood and reached for a knife to cut the lop-sided tower of cake. Buried beneath the slightly burned crust were clusters of nuts and juice berries. She placed a thick slice on Desmond's trencher. He cast her a look of dismay, but at a glower from her he took a tentative bite.

A look of surprise covered his face, and he took a bigger bite.

Curious, Thea cut a piece for Dahlabar and then one for herself. She felt Dahlabar's gaze upon her as she took a bite. She smiled as the tastes of cinnamon and vanilla filled her mouth.

The icing was made of clabbered cream and honey. No wonder it had been sliding off the cake's sides. "This is wonderful, poppa-Dah." She watched Dahlabar grin with pleasure.

"The baker's widowed daughter showed me how," he said. "Eat. Eat more."

She did not have to be coaxed twice. She finished the slice and then another. Desmond and Dahlabar went two beyond hers.

*****

Desmond pushed back from the table. "I could not eat a mouthful more."

Thea reached for the pitcher. "More wine?"

The mage shook his head.

"Poppa-Dah?"

"No. I must rise early to see our guestreturned to his school."

Thea began to clear the table. Dahlabar laid

his hand over hers. "Not this eve, daughter. I will see to it. Go to bed."

"But I'm not tired." A yawn surprised her and she smiled as she covered her mouth with her hand. It had been a long day, but she hated to see the celebration draw to an end. She dared a quick look at Desmond. Tomorrow he returned to the Mage School. Would she ever see him again? A sudden sadness made her sigh, and she stood. "I will say goodnight."

Desmond stood, and then winced. "Good sleep, Thea."

She stared at him for a moment. "And you." She walked to the loft's ladder.

*****

Thea awoke to voices, and for a moment wondered whom it was that Dahlabar spoke to, and then remembered the day before and Desmond. They would not leave without first seeing her?

She kicked the coverings aside and pulled her new gown on. Forgetting her boots, she hurried down the ladder and out the cottage's open door. Two heads swiveled toward her.

Dahlabar had hitched their pony to the cart and Desmond sat upon the seat.

"Morning, lazy bumpkin. I was just going to wake you," Dahlabar said.

She combed her fingers through her unbound hair. "Did you break your fast?"

Dahlabar grinned. "We finished off the cake."

"You hair shines like molten gold," Desmond said.

"What?" His words had been so low, she was not sure she had heard them.

"Nothing." He reached for the reins.

"Not so quick, lad," Dahlabar said and hopped into the seat beside the mage. "I will do the guiding. Maple is getting on in years, and I will not see her tired."

Desmond looked at her to Dahlabar and then focused his attention in the air between the pony's ears. "I would like to visit again if I could."

"What?" Dahlabar said.

"I would like to visit again."

She held her breath as she waited for Dahlabar's response, then released it as he said. "You are welcome, young mage." He jiggled the reins and Maple moved forward. Desmond did not meet her gaze as the cart moved past. She felt a quick prick of irritation that was salved as the young mage turned and looked back as they exited the clearing.

*****

Desmond became a regular visitor and their friendship grew. At first the young mage came only when he knew Dahlabar would be there, but then he changed to times when he must have known she would be alone.

They walked together in the woods, and he told her of the lessons he learned at the Mage School, of scrolls and their spells that made her heart yearn to see them herself.

She told him of the animals she spoke to and healed, and of the far off lands they had journeyed from.

Today they again walked, but after Desmond helped her cross a wide log, he did not release her captured hand. Instead he pulled her close and kissed her. It did not surprise her. She had felt it coming. What did give her a start was the familiarity

of the feel of his mouth upon hers. We have done this before. The thought came sure and strong. But how? Then she remembered last night's dream, the two of them together, their naked bodies locked together in passion, but not in these forms.

The memory made her heart beat fast and she pressed tightly against him. He stilled gripped her hand, but now released it to slip his arms around her waist and draw her closer still.

His lips left hers to kiss their way down her throat. She moaned and lay back in his arms. "I love you, Thea," he murmured against the pulse that throbbed in her neck.

Her hands rose to clasp his shoulders and she felt his leave her waist and rise to cup her breasts. She gasped as her nipples hardened. He raised his head to look into her eyes. "I want to be with you always. Come to the Mage School with me. I have already spoken to them of you."

"What?" She stepped back from him. The words sent a chill through her.

"Buried in the woods is no place for a woman of such power."

She examined his face and saw only pleading and love. "What of those who need me? Who will care for them when they are in pain?"

He tried to draw her close again. "I need you."

Thea stepped back further from him. "And what of Dahlabar?"

Desmond frowned. "I have asked of Dahlabar. I know his and your story. When first he came, he told the king he would return to his land when the time was right."

"No," Thea gasped.

Desmond grabbed her hands and drew her

close. "You are no longer a child. You are a woman, with a woman's needs. Release him to return to his home."

She shook her head. "You say he stays because of me? That he wishes to go?"

"Thea..."

"Dahlabar has told you this?"

"What have I told?" Dahlabar came from the trees.

She whirled to face him. "Do you wish to leave me, poppa-Dah? Does your first home call to you?"

Dahlabar frowned. "What is this you say?" She watched him look from her to Desmond and then back.

Desmond stepped up beside her and squared his shoulders.

"I have asked Thea to join me at the Mage School. I love her."

"That is not my daughter's path."

"Who are you to say?" Desmond demanded.

"The Goddess has blessed Thea..."

"She has it within her to do more than heal animals." Desmond's voice held scorn. "We can train her to use the power within her."

For the first time in all of her years, she watched Dahlabar's eyes kindle with rage. "You think healing is beneath her?" His voice was a blade, slicing sharp with each word.

Desmond paled, but did not back down. "You have taught her what you can, but it is time the fledgling left the nest."

"You braying ass," Dahlabar said, stepping toward Desmond.

"No," she said, coming between them. "The choice is mine." She looked from one man to the

other. "Is it not?"

Desmond stared at her. "Choice? I have laid my heart before you. And you love me. I see it. Why is there a choice to be made?"

She held her hand out toward him. "But I first loved my father and the Goddess."

"I trusted you with my daughter. Welcomed you to my hearth," Dahlabar said. "and you have trampled both beneath your boots. Get out of my sight." He put his hand around Thea's shoulders. "Let's go home, daughter."

She twisted away from him. "I have not told my decision."

Dahlabar glared at Desmond. "He is no longer welcome in my home."

"It's my home too," Thea said.

Desmond moved toward her. "It need not be."

Dahlabar stepped in front of him. "Do not touch her."

"Out of my way," Desmond demanded, adding, "do not force me to use my magic to make you do so."

"Enough," Thea cried. "I will not have this." She turned and, with a strangled sob, dashed into the trees.

"Thea."

"Daughter."

Their words trailed her, but she did not lessen her forward fleeing. Anger led speed to her feet and on she ran, heedless of the direction she took. Around trees and over rocks she fled, splashed through first one stream and then another. At last, when her legs would take her no further, she stopped and collapsed upon a flat-topped boulder. Her chest heaving, she looked around. Where was

she? She listened for pursers, but all was quiet. As she breathed and willed her heart to slow its beat, the forest became alive once more around her with the trill of birdsong.

She closed her eyes and relived Dahlabar and Desmond's angry words. Tears filled her eyes and ran down her cheeks. How could they ask her to choose between them?

She wiped at her face and eyes and looked around again. Nothing was familiar. A hunting bird cried out and she shivered and rubbed her arms.Night was falling and she was not dressed to spend it unsheltered beneath the stars.

"It is time, Chosen One. Come to me."

The words rang in her head and she scrambled to her feet and looked wildly around. "Who are you? Show yourself."

"You know me, Thea. Now follow my words."

"Goddess?"

"I will care for you, daughter. It is time for you to know your path."

"You will guide me home?"

"Your journey does not take you back."

"But what of father? He will fear for me," Thea said, even as her footsteps took her forward.

"Dahlabar and Desmond will know you are safe. Now listen, daughter. This is where you must go."

*****

For five days Thea followed the Goddess' words, walking deeper and deeper into the forest. The sixth morning found her before a mountain, its peak lost among the clouds. A path led upward.

"Climb," the Goddess said.

Her feet sure, Thea followed the twisting

route. When the sun rode high, she saw it, a dark hole in the mountain's wall.

"Am I to go in?"No answering words came to her.

From within the cave came the soft sigh of wind brushing treetops. She peered into the blackness and as she watched, a flame flared and then vanished. What was that? As she stared it flickered once more. Curiosity surfaced, but still she hesitated. Overhead, thunder rumbled, and then a fat drop of rain pelted her head. It was followed by another and then another. With an annoyed shrug she entered the cave. Why would the Goddess bring her this far, only to let her die?

She moved toward the flame, deeper and deeper into the cave, until the opening behind her became nothing but a small hole. The walls around her began to glow a soft golden-green. The soft sighing she heard earlier was now a throaty rumble. She had been trailing her fingers along the cave's wall, and with her next step her hand found nothing.

Thea stopped and took a deep breath. The sound echoed back from the chamber before her, and even with the walls surrounding her glowing brighter, its top was lost in the darkness above. A boulder the size of a small mountain rose from the middle of the cavernous room. As she watched, its sides heaved and the throaty rumble again filled the area. "By the Goddess," she whispered, and then gasped as a flame flared from the boulder's farthest end. At her gasp, a window in the boulder opened. Thea blinked and knuckled her eyes.

No, not a window, an eye. A voice, warm as the sun's kiss and sweet as fire-bush honey, flowed into her mind.

"*At last, Chosen, you are here. I am Zara,*

avatar to the Goddess. Come forward and hear my words."

Part Four

Thea looked skyward. It should be time for Zara to return from her hunt. She and the dragon had been together now eleven sunrises. The first night and on into the next day, Zara had told her she was to be the Goddess's mortal. That she had been blessed with the ability to not only speak to mortal creatures, but also to be understood, and to understand those of magic, and this would aid her in the Goddess' wish: an end to Daradawn's strife.

She had listened to the dragon in silence, accepting all said, but a fear grew inside her. How was she to stop dwarf from hating fairie, and elf from despising man?

When she voiced her fears, Zara's rage rang in her head. *"They will be made to listen. It is the Goddess' will. Our first visits will be to the villages of men. The word of us will spread."*

She thought of the priests of the Temple of Ogdah and took a sudden delight in imagining their faces as she and the golden dragon landed among them.

"I ask first that I be allowed to seek out my father and Desmond. They must hear of my decision from my own lips."

"It will be as you desire, Thea," Zara mind-sent, and plans were made to journey to her home village this day.

*****

A shadow floated across the valley and she looked up. Zara flew between her and the sun. As she watched, the dragon glided downward in a slow

spiral and, at the last moment, back-winged and floated to the ground like an enormous butterfly. Thea's stomach knotted. They had talked of how she was to ride the dragon's back. Behind the great head, spine ridges began, and she was to seat herself between two of the ridges. She understood the plan, but had yet to mount the dragon.

Zara turned her golden eyes upon Thea. Her mind-voice came, sated and smug. *"We fly?"*

"Yes."

The dragon extended her right front leg. Taking a deep breath, Thea walked to it. The dragon's scales were slick beneath her boots, and Thea slipped and slid backwards.

"Remove them," Zara sent.

Balancing on one foot, she pulled first one and then the other boot free. Holding the boots in her hand she looked up the length of the extended leg.

"Mount, Thea."

She placed her foot upon the leg, just above the first talon. The scales were warm against her skin, their pattern altering from slick to grainy and then back to slick as she climbed the gentle incline. Behind the dragon's head, Thea gathered her skirts above her knees and straddled the first spine ridge. She fit easily between the ridges, but blessed the bundled skirt beneath her bottom.

"You are ready?"

"I am." Thea placed her boots upon her lap.

Dirt and leaves gusted as Zara flapped her wings. Thea leaned forward and shielded her face against the neck ridge before her. A jolt vibrated up her spine, almost knocking her teeth together. It was followed by another and then another, then her stomach lurched.

Surprised, she sat back and opened her eyes.

Wind gusted into her face and blew the hair that had escaped her braid straight out behind her. Out of the corner of her right eye she caught movement and turned her head in time to see the great wings stroke downward. Zara's body rose with the movement and Thea bounced upward. With a shriek, she wrapped her arms around the spiny hump before her. The sudden movement sent her boots sliding from her lap and she watched them tumble downward.

"I am sorry, Thea." Zara's mind-voice was ripe with amusement. *"In time this will become easier for both of us."*

Unable to form a thought, Thea watched the trees and streams grow small beneath her. Then Zara skimmed a mountain's peak and there was nothing left in Thea's mind but awe-filled wonder.

Above the mountain, the dragon spread her wings and they glided, first up and then down.

"How do you do so?" Thea asked.

"I ride the air," Zara said.

All too soon, a village neared beneath them. Thea leaned to the side and looked down. It was hers. From the sky view it was easy to see the Temple of Ogdah rising from the village's center, the shops and homes clustered around it like a hen with chicks. Only one other structure challenged the temple's stature, and it on the far end of the village, the Mage School. All below was vacant and still.

As she watched, the first bells of morn pealed from the temple tower, summoning the priests to early prayers.

"Were will we land?" she sent to the dragon.

"Beyond is a wide valley. Brace yourself. I fly higher to hide among the clouds. It would not do to

send those below into a panic."

Zara circled downward. At first Thea watched, but then closed her eyes as the continuing movement made her stomach pitch.

"Hold, Thea."

And then a jolt jerked her head back, quickly followed by the spine-jarring thuds.

"We are here." Zara sent.

Thea opened her eyes. As she stood, she realized her hands and face were stiff with cold. Gloves and something to shield her skin would be needed before she rode dragon-back again.

On the ground, she looked around. She knew this valley. Dahlabar's cottage lay just beyond the ridge.

The cottage looked the same as she neared the closed door. Her palm ready to press it inward, she stopped and knocked instead. There was no answer. Where was her Poppa-Dah? She tried to recall what day this was, but had no idea. Could he be in the village?

Tempted to go inside, she instead turned away. The cottage felt hers no longer, and an ache formed in her stomach. Fighting tears, she walked around to the lean-to. The cart and Maple the pony were gone.

She winced as she stepped on a stone and sighed at the thought of the walk ahead of her. First she'd find Dahlabar, and then boots, gloves and warm coverings for her arms and legs. But what of Desmond, a voice asked. If the Goddess wills it, then we shall see, she answered and began her walk.

The village was just waking as she entered the square. Yawning farmers unloaded wagons,

preparing for the day's hawking of goods. Thea kept her head down and, ignoring the stares at her bare feet, headed toward the bakery. It was where Dahlabar always went first.

She heard his voice while still outside the shop's door. "A full scheckle? That is robbery."

The bartering had reached its ending She smiled. A full scheckle it had been for their seven days worth of bread and rolls for the past three summers, and a full scheckle it would continue to be, but both the baker and Dahlabar so enjoyed playing out the scene.

Conscious of her wind-whipped hair and rumpled gown, she stepped into the shadows of an ally and waited. She heard his humming as he neared and called. "Poppa-Dah."

Dahlabar halted, then peered into the dimness. Trembling, Thea stepped into the sunlight.

He said nothing, just stared into her face for a long moment and then dropped the paper-wrapped bundle and opened his arms wide.

With a small cry, she jumped into them and felt them close around her. "Poppa-Dah," she forced by the lump in her throat. "I am sorry."

He pressed her back and looked into her face. "Do not cry, daughter, and do not make apologies to me. It was I who sent you fleeing. It was not my right to force your path."

"It was the Goddess' will," she said. "If I had not fled I would have not learned of her plans for me."

"What has the Goddess shown you?"

"Her avatar, Zara. She waits for me in the valley beyond your cottage." She felt tears threaten.

"I have come to tell you and Desmond, and then I will be off. Popp-Dah, I don't know when I will return."

"I understand, daughter, but I will miss your sorely. How will you and the avatar travel? Afoot?"

She shook her head with a shaky smile. "Zara is a..."

"Thea?" The voice came from behind them and they both turned.

"Desmond." Love coursed through her and she took a step toward him.

The young mage stepped back, avoided her outstretched hand. "You have returned."

She dropped her hand as she nodded, hurt left her unable to form a word. Was this the way it was to be? She had yearned to see him, but now? What would his reaction be at her leaving once more? She had thought their love strong enough, but now doubt left a cold lump in her stomach.

"What have you decided?" Desmond said. "You've had over twelve sunrises to do so. Do you come to be with me at the Mage School?"

She shook her head. "Desmond..."

But he cut off her words as a red flush rose into his cheeks. Desmond whipped around to glare at Dahlabar. "This is your fault, old man. You seek to tie her to you."

Her father sighed. "No. This is not what I wished, but I feared it would become so."

The young mage looked puzzled. "I don't understand."

As Thea started to speak, Zara's words entered her mind. *We fly?*

"One moment more," she said, "then we will leave."

At her words, Dahlabar's eyes glistened with tears.

"To whom do you speak, Thea?" Desmond said. "You do not stay with me or go with Dahlabar?"

She held her hand out toward him again. "I have come back to say good-bye for a while..."

"What do you mean? You love me."

"The Goddess requires me to walk another path..."

She watched the blood leave Desmond's face. He grabbed her hands and pulled her toward him. "No, I won't let you go. You can serve the Goddess here. You have done so these many years. I was selfish. I care not that you remain at the cottage with your father."

"Desmond, I..."

Zara's voice came again. *"Thea."*

"I'm coming."

"What is wrong?" Desmond said. "To whom do you speak?" He repeated the question.

"The dragon," she said.

The mage dropped her hands and stepped back. "A dragon?" He looked from her face and into Dahlabar's. "Your daughter is ill. We must take her to the Mage School. They will heal her mind."

Thea frowned in exasperation. "I am not ill. My mind is fine. Zara is the Goddess' avatar. She aids me in my journey..."

Desmond did not wait for her to finish her words. "No one can speak to a dragon."

"She hears me in her mind, and I her," Thea said. "She brought me here upon her back."

"No," Desmond said and grabbed her by her shoulders. "We will help you."

Aftermath

Zara's roar of outrage made Thea scream and drop to her knees.

"Dahlabar, help me," Desmond said. "We must take her to the mages."

"Let go of me," Thea said. "Do you wish the dragon to come?" She saw Desmond's hesitancy and rushed on. "I will take you to Zara. Will that convince you that I am in my right mind?"

The mage shook his head. "But how can it be..." he murmured as Dahlabar helped her to her feet.

"I will show you, but first I must make a few purchases."

*****

New boots upon her feet, Thea told them of her journey as she led them toward the valley. Dahlabar asked questions, but Desmond remained quiet. She felt his gaze on her as they walked. What went through his mind? Could their love withstand the separation, or was this the end?

"We come," she sent ahead to Zara.

They stopped behind the shelter of a tree. "Wait here," Thea said. "I don't know how Zara will react to strangers." She did not wait for their response, but turned and walked from them.

The dragon stood in the middle of the valley. She tossed her head as she saw Thea. *"We go."*

The words were not a question, but an order, laced with impatience.

"Please, Zara. These men are important to me."

The dragon's gusty sigh lifted Thea's hair, even from across the valley. *"Bring them."*

Thea turned back toward the trees. "Okay. But stay beside me."

She heard their footsteps, but did not turn.

"By the Goddess," Dahlabar said in awe. "She is beautiful."

Zara trumpeted in pleased response.

Thea turned to face Desmond. He said nothing, just stared at the golden dragon.

At last he turned to her. "You can speak to it?"

Thea nodded.

She watched him close his eyes for a moment and his face twisted in pain.

"What does she want from you? Your Goddess."

She reached to touch his arm. "I must go from you for a while." She felt his arm tense beneath her fingers.

"I love you, Thea. I want us to have a life together. A home and children."

"I want that also," she said. "And we will have it, just not for a while."

Desmond clasped her hands. "If you leave, it will not happen. I know this in my soul."

She smiled. "I will return. The Goddess has promised me this. Then we will be together."

A sad smile curved Desmond's lips. "Swear to me," he said, "that you will always love me, that you will seek me throughout eternity."

Thea laughed softly. "Desmond, I will always love you..."

"Swear," he said, his hands tightening upon hers.

"I swear," she whispered, a sudden chill making her shiver. "Desmond, what have you foreseen? You are not a far-viewer."

He dropped her hands and turned from her. "I have seen nothing."

"*Thea.*" Zara's mind touched hers, but this

time gentle with understanding. "*We must go.*"

"I must leave," Thea said, and she heard Desmond sigh as he faced her. He opened his arms and she went into them. He pulled her close and she listened to his heartbeat beneath her cheek.

She felt him kiss the top of her head and she pulled back and looked into his eyes. Her lips parted to speak, but he lowered his head and pressed his lips against hers. Their kiss was long and deep. She felt tears spring into her eyes. Why do I feel as if we are saying good bye? We are not. I will return.

Desmond stepped back from her, and without another word, turned and walked away. Before the first tree, he stopped and looked back. "Remember your promise. Always seek me. I will love you for eternity."

She lifted a hand toward him, but he turned and moved into the trees. "Desmond," she whispered.

"You must follow your path, daughter," Dahlabar said from beside her.

She closed her eyes and swallowed the tears in her throat. "We will be together. We will." There was no response, and she opened her eyes and looked into her father's face. "I will miss you, Poppa-Dah."

"And I you. But I know the Goddess will protect you..." A roar filled the air. "As well as the dragon," he added.

She rose up onto her toes and kissed his cheek. "It is time."

"Go. I will be here when you return."

She turned and walked from him. Zara extended her leg as she neared. Thea pulled her new boots from her feet and placed them in the

woven bag atop her other purchases. She could stand another short flight without the warm leggings and woolen tunic. The bag had two strong ties and, with the boots inside, she wrapped the lengths of woven cloth around her waist and knotted them.

Boots secure, she climbed the dragon's leg, seated herself between the first two neckline ridges, and pulled on the leather gloves. She turned and looked across the valley at Dahlabar. He lifted his hand and waved.

"Are you ready, Thea?" Zara sent.

Unable to speak past the lump in her throat, she nodded.

The dragon took three lumbering steps, and then leapt. Dirt and grass rose as her huge wings beat against the air. Thea buried her head against the spinney ridge in front of her and felt her stomach dip with each sweep of Zara's wings. When she opened her eyes and looked down, the valley was far below and Dahlabar but a toy-sized man. As Zara winged away, he still stood, stared upward, and Thea watched until she could see him no more.

As they neared a mountain's side, Thea turned and faced forward, her gaze on the land spread before her. *"What now?"* she sent to Zara.

"I know not. The Goddess will show us the way." And with those words, the dragon dipped a wing and glided onward.

About the Author

Barbara M. Hodges lives on the central coast of California. She shares her life with husband Jeff, two basset hounds, Ophelia and Hamlet, as well as with a sassy ginger-striped feline, Wallace.

Barbara is a big NASCAR fan and enjoys watching the sport on television, as well as getting away to see the races in person.

Website: barbaramhodges.com
Email: bassetbarb@aol.com

www.ingramcontent.com/pod-product-compliance
Lightning Source LLC
Chambersburg PA
CBHW050943120626
46552CB00001B/358